THE
NOT-SO-SILENT
PASSAGE

THE
NOT-SO-SILENT
PASSAGE

how to manage your man's
menopause*

CHERYL SOLIMINI

* without committing manslaughter

GIBBS·SMITH
P
PUBLISHER

SALT LAKE CITY

First edition

99 98 5 4 3 2 1

This is a Peregrine Smith Book, published by
Gibbs Smith, Publisher
P.O. Box 667
Layton, Utah 84041

Design by Cheryl Solimini
Printed and bound in the U.S.A.

Library of Congress Cataloging-in-Publication Data
Solimini, Cheryl
The not-so-silent passage: how to manage your man's menopause
without committing manslaughter / by Cheryl Solimini.
c. pm.
ISBN 0-87905-751-3
1. Middle-aged men—Psychology—Humor. 2 Midlife crisis—Humor.
3. Man-woman relationships—Humor. I Title.
PN623.M47S65 1998
818'.5402-dc21 97-29018
CIP

For Martin—as always, the exception

For Mom—don't read pages 25-29, 57-58 and Chapter 6.

———————

Special thanks to Bernard Kruger, M.D., New York City internist and testosterone aficionado, who provided "some stimulation and a little bit of help"

Contents

ACKNOWLEDGEMENTS   ix

FOREWORD   xi

1. GOING THROUGH "THE CHANGE"
(YEAH, WE'RE TALKING TO *YOU,* BUDDY)   1

    Up, Up and Away   1

    The French Have a Word for It   3

    Iron John, Meet Tupperware Phil   4

    The Unforgiven   7

    Attorneys on Ice,
       Butchers in the Operating Room   8

    The Andropausal Man in the Media   11

    Just the F.A.Q.s, Ma'am   13

2. MEN: THE AWKWARD YEARS (BIRTH TO DEATH)   16

    Born to Be Wild   17

    Fire in the Belly—Where's the Mylanta?   19

    Guns: A Boy's Best Friend   20

    Is That a Subpoena in Your Pocket or
       Are You Just Happy to See Me?   21

    Turn Right at the Next Vector   22

    To Every Thingamajig There Is a Season   24

    Everything He Needs to Know He Learned
       in Junior High   25

    The One-Eyed Worm   29

    You Just Don't Understand . . .
       Hey! Are You Even Listening to Me?   30

3. MEN ARE FROM MARS . . . WOMEN JUST WISH THEY'D REMEMBER TO PICK UP THE DRY CLEANING ON THEIR WAY BACK TO EARTH   32
> Is He Losing It? Test His Testosterone   33
> The 10 Warning Signs of Andropause   36

4. THE TOYS OF AUTUMN: ACCESSORIZING FOR ANDROPAUSE   44
> Auto Eroticism   45
> Team Player   46
> Hair Apparent (Men Behaving Baldly)   47
> Waiting to Inhale   52
> Bigger, Longer, Wider   53
> The Family Jewels   55

5. SMART MEN, FOOLISH HORMONES   57

6. HIS WILLY, HIS SELF   68
> I Am Joe's Rapidly Decaying Body   71
> Fixing Mr. Fix-It   73

7. I'M OKAY—YOU, ON THE OTHER HAND, NEED LOTS OF HELP: WHAT YOU CAN DO FOR HIM/ WHAT HE CAN DO TO HIMSELF   76
> To Make Him Feel . . . More Virile   78
> . . . Less Bald   79
> . . . Less Old   80

8. CAVEAT BIMBO: WOMEN WHO LOVE MEN WHO LEAVE THEM FOR YOUNGER WOMEN WHO MAKE THESE MEN LOOK LIKE IDIOTS   82
> Signs That He May Be Interested in a Younger Woman   85
> The Fools: Untested Secrets for Recapturing the Heart of Mr. Good-Enough   87

BACKWORD   91

Acknowledgements

My gratitude to those who shared their witticisms, criticisms and encouragement, including (in alphabetical order only): my editor, Madge Baird; Sylvia Barsotti; Barbara Carlin; Phyllis Celentano; Eileen Fallon; Louise Fiore; the Forsythes; MaryPat Hyland; Joan of Santa Barbara; Linda Konner, my agent and godmother; the Kurtz-Bernards; Joanne Morici; the Mourases; Laurie Nikolski; the Silvermans; Meryl and Andrew Solimini and Beck; Steve Solimini; the United Cousins Network; and the yentas at *menopause.support.alt*. And regards to newspaper columnist Ann Landers and radio personality Howard Stern, whose public forums provide invaluable insight into the male mind.

Foreword

*T*hanks to Gail Sheehy's *The Silent Passage,* the 40 million American women who will pass through menopause within the next two decades will be armed with a greater sense of self-esteem, a feeling of control over their own biological destiny and the name of at least one good gynecologist.

Sure, this will be a time of difficult physical as well as emotional transition for many of us, but menopause has its upsides:

•Once the biological responsibility of childbearing has passed, you will be free to become Attorney General of the United States or Prime Minister of England.

•When you say, tearfully, to a man in a crowded restaurant, "My friend is late," she really *is* late and *he's* the maître d' who won't change your dinner reservation to 7:30.

•You'll never again have to think twice before putting on a pair of white pants.

Yet these advantages are meaningless for those of us who have to live with any of the 38 million men who will be experiencing their own "change of life" during the same period.

Hot flashes? You can always turn on the fan. Night sweats? Kick off the sheets. Mood swings? Enjoy the ride.

But how do you cope when your husband of 32 years takes up with the countergirl at Dairy Queen? Announces he's quit his job as a junk-bond trader to run a fishing charter out of Key West? Comes home wearing a toupee that looks like a shag-carpet sample? Or worse yet, orders a 100% cotton twill bush jacket from the J. Peterman catalog and goes off to find his "Inner Stallone"? By now, you may want to trade in your 50-year-old for two 25s (if he hasn't already beaten you to it).

As is evident in child-custody settlements, tabloid headlines and *The First Wives Club*, it is *women* who suffer most from men's middle age. That's why you—as a first, second, or I-just-want-to-be-*last* wife—need to gather as much information as you can about this stage of your man's life. Once you understand what he is going through, you can sympathize with it, prepare for the inevitable and, as a show of faith, put Ivana Trump's *and* Marla Maples' divorce lawyers on retainer.

As usual, women have to help their men, because, let's face it, men can't help themselves (except to their clients' trust funds, your kid's baby-sitter or the last of the good Scotch). And now they have a new excuse: It has recently been discovered that middle-aged males, like women at menopause, are merely victims of their no-longer-raging hormones.

That's right. Medical scientists finally admit that there *is* a "male menopause." Until now, the highly complex, self-destructive and ridiculous behaviors exhibited by the middle-aged man were patronizingly referred to as "midlife crisis."[1] Now research has confirmed that it is a series of serious, escalating and devastating biological changes that bring about those highly complex, self-destructive and ridiculous behaviors.[2]

As you'll learn, men's levels of testosterone, like women's levels of estrogen, take a dive with age. When this hormone loses potency, a middle-aged man is like a one-armed war veteran who can still feel his amputated limb but can no longer do push-ups. But with this new medical understanding, men can now blame it all on their hormones, just as women since Eve have done. Of course, the danger is that they will take even less responsibility for their actions than ever before.

---

[1]Not to be confused with his "midmorning crisis," his "postprandial crisis," his "how did this dent get in the car? crisis" and a myriad of other panic attacks that enrich his day—and yours.

[2]Most of the medical research that will be presented throughout this book is true. The rest was made up to be amusing, but also to prove a point—that medical research requires too much time and money.

WIFE arrives home to find HUSBAND naked and
having his toenails painted by perky door-to-
door cosmetics SALESWOMAN, also naked.

WIFE [*to Husband*]: What do we have here?

HUSBAND [*to Wife*]: I can explain! I was having
a . . . a hot flash. Yeah, that's right. So I took
off all my clothes. Then she came to the door,
and just to be polite . . .

WIFE [*to Saleswoman*]: No, I mean the polish.
Is that Sun-kissed Apricot? I'll take a bottle.

SALESWOMAN [*to all*]: YES! That's my mil-
lionth sale! The pink Cadillac is MINE!

Adding to the difficulty at this vulnerable stage in his
life is that your man is totally unaware his behavior is out
of the ordinary. You, of course, are too loyal—and speech-
less—to mention it. When I brought up the subject of
male menopause in the exhaustive interviews I conducted across the country,[3] the men crossed their legs,
turned their heads, coughed and denied that they were
going through *anything.* In the meantime, their wives were in
the bedroom going through their husbands' pockets and
credit-card receipts, looking for evidence to the contrary.

Even men with little to feel guilty about deny any midlife
changes in behavior. For instance, I wrote to my friend Alicia[4] asking if she had any anecdotes about her 40ish husband, Jeff, the vice president of a public-relations firm. I
received a reply within days. She apologized, saying she had
planned to tell me about Jeff's sudden interest in fast cars,
but, unfortunately, this thoughtful and honorable (not to
mention handsome) man[5] saw my note and inquired calmly,
"WHY WOULD THERE BE ANY ANECDOTES ABOUT *ME*?!?!"

---

[3]Actually, just everyone on my Friends & Family calling plan.

[4]Throughout, the names, locations and/or occupations of my respondents
have been disguised to avoid violation of their privacy.

[5]Allison—oops, I mean *Alicia:* I hope this placates Jim...uh, *Jeff,* so that he
won't be too upset over this violation of his privacy.

(Then Jeff grabbed his crash helmet, climbed into his Trans Am and sped away. Not really.) My friend's letter ended with, "Well, I have to live with him, so I pretended to be equally astounded by the inference. End of story."

Why this conspiracy of silence? We women certainly aren't immune to similar midlife anxieties and medical symptoms, particularly now that we can "have it all"—career, family and a heart attack before age 50. The difference is that we don't mind talking, writing or forming support groups about our problems. If not for our willingness to bring our private turmoil out in the open, Phil Donahue and Oprah Winfrey would be on welfare.

And in the process, we share solutions. For instance, when Linda is once again passed over for promotion to vice president and her teenage children will communicate with her only via their Web page, she wonders, "Is that all there is?" But she says it out loud, to Madge. Madge laughs and says, "Oh, I went through that 6 months ago. You'll get over it. Have some ginseng tea." Thus, Linda is reassured that her feeling of hopelessness, like her premenstrual bloat, is just temporary. Does she go around the corner for a pack of cigarettes, never to return home? No, she goes around to the salon for a facial, maybe even a foot massage, and feels much, much better.

A man, on the other hand, rarely shares such concerns with himself and never, ever shares them with another man. Faced with the signs of aging and with anxiety about his place in the world, he is convinced he is the only person on the planet who has ever felt this way. He thinks these feelings Must Mean Something. He thinks that he must pay attention to them and obey whatever irrational commands are being barked out by his testosterone-impaired brain—which has a voice that sounds remarkably like Barry White. In other words, he has stopped thinking completely. He should only be pitied—or perhaps locked in the basement, where the only harm he can do is to tinker around his workbench and build a bookshelf that falls over when you try to put actual books on it.

A woman finds it hard to believe that her man wouldn't want to explore his disturbing feelings, analyze their causes and perhaps fix them (even though he might not have the right tools and will have to go back to the hardware store twice). But history tells us that men don't really operate that way. For proof, visit any public bathroom.

They were designed by men—we know that by the number of receptacles in men's rooms versus the stalls in ladies' rooms. Obviously, the guys at the construction site gave themselves extra watering holes because they didn't want to waste time in the bathroom. They prefer wasting time lying on scaffolding, whistling at female passersby and scratching themselves. The foreman, wanting to cut expenses so he could embezzle the difference from his overinflated construction estimate, invented the urinal.

But it's obvious that these men didn't think ahead. They forgot that they might have to use these disposal units again, in front of strangers. My independent inquiries confirm that no male is really comfortable urinating next to a man he doesn't know and would not recognize after this moment because his eyes are riveted on the wall in front of him. (Luckily, the wall is covered with distracting reading matter, like "Elvis is alive and well and living in your colon"[6] or "If you're reading this, you must be pissing on your shoes.") He's even less comfortable urinating next to a man he *does* know. But because he won't admit he was wrong, urinals continue to be included in lavatory blueprints across the country.

Except at home. And that's where urinals would really be useful. They would greatly reduce the number of domestic accidents—as when a wife reminds her husband that if he keeps forgetting to put down the toilet seat after he's done, she'll "accidentally" forget to have sex with him.

The bottom line: Men don't want to find out something's wrong. Then they might have to change it.

---

[6]Still on view in the railroad-terminal men's room in Hoboken, New Jersey.

Perhaps we women expect too much from this generation of men, just because they survived Vietnam, the women's movement and the disco era. After all, someone who would wear *that* shirt with *that* tie can't have too much self-awareness. You, as the wife,[7] are more likely to spot The Change in your aging partner and won't be able to ignore it or the mess it makes. Cheer up! This, too, shall pass—once his will is in probate.

If we all try to educate ourselves and our men, perhaps we can help them avoid the missteps of middle-aged men past. Perhaps if Woody Allen had been helped to identify the source of his inner turmoil, he would have gone out to pick up some powdered elk antlers (see Chapter 6) instead of his girlfriend's 19-year-old daughter. Perhaps Senator Bob Packwood wouldn't have needed to keep a diary if he had accepted his failing memory as a middle-aged perk of his position ("I'm sorry, Mr. Chairman of the Ethics Committee, I either disremember or can't recall at that moment in time groping Miss Smith"). Perhaps if certain major-league sportscasters hadn't taken their sex lives into extra innings, the whole country wouldn't have heard the play-by-play of their playing around. And only good taste, and the threat of a lawsuit involving more attorneys than currently serve on the Supreme Court, could prevent us from drawing the obvious conclusion: that what really happened on O.J. Simpson's Brentwood estate was directly related to the state of O.J.'s "bent woody."

Chances are, those guys still wouldn't think what they did was wrong. But if we had realized that these men's extreme reactions to middle age were, in some ways, beyond their control, decent people—and journalists on all seven continents—might have been less quick to judge them.

---

[7]Of course, this advice also applies if you are his lover, significant other or one-night stand, but for convenience, it will be assumed that you and your man have a spousal relationship, and the terms "wife" and "husband" will be used throughout this book. However, if you are not legally married, get out now and don't look back!

Our ultimate goal, of course, should be to find a cure for male menopause. It is hoped that this book will bring this debilitating condition to public attention and inspire others, on the grassroots level, to hold fund-raising events (maybe a Willie Nelson concert) so that the needed research could be financed. Perhaps a celebrity who has had many personal contacts with menopausal males—I have in mind Elizabeth Taylor—could take up the cause and make this a charity every woman could write off.

In the meantime, though, we must do what we can to deal with our menopausal men: laugh at them.

1

Going Through "The Change" (Yeah, We're Talking to *You*, Buddy)

I wanted to achieve some distinction in my life. I think most people do. This is the way I've chosen to do it—to find a very interesting project, something that is difficult, that is a high goal, and then figure out how to do it.

*T*he 52-year-old man speaking above is referring to:
  a. His relentless search for a cure for Chronic Fatigue Syndrome.
  b. His selfless decision to follow in the late Mother Teresa's footsteps.
  c. His witless attempt to float around the world in a balloon.

Up, Up and Away

If you answered *c*, then you were watching *Nightline* on January 21, 1997. The week before, an American securities trader, a Swiss psychiatrist and a British businessman[8] took to the sky in considerably larger and more sophisticated versions of a child's birthday-party favor. Note that they each went in *separate* balloons and thus could not take advantage

---

[8]Doesn't this sound like the beginning of a joke that ends with the punchline, "I thought *you* brought the hot air"? It's not.

of the air-traffic diamond lane during rush hour. Note, too, that these three men were old enough to get dizzy just *blowing up* a balloon.

Each excursion required months of preparation time and tens of thousands of dollars in the latest balloon-onautics technology. Unfortunately, two of the balloons were forced down by technical difficulties in less than a day. But the lone American drifted at 18,000 to 24,000 feet above the Earth's surface, zipping along at 65 to 120 miles per hour, for a week. He had trained for this airborne adventure for a year, acclimating his body to the high altitude by using a home decompression chamber.[9] During the actual flight, he slept about two hours a night, ate military rations, endured freezing temperatures and peed in a bucket—all tests of his mettle that he could just as easily have experienced at a maternity hospital closer to home.

Though this man did not, ultimately, make it around the world, he did set world records for endurance and distance for a balloon flight—and for holding his bladder (after a week, there's only so much that will fit into a bucket). So he did "achieve some distinction." However, most women, especially those who have enjoyed more than one stay in a maternity hospital, would assume he just wanted to get out of the house. More likely, he didn't want to take his turn driving the kids' car pool. In fact, during this particular balloonist's seven days in the stratosphere, a roomful of similarly middle-aged and sparse-haired men worked round the clock, hunched over computer tracking terminals, communicating by modem to guide him around the hostile airspace over Libya[10] so he wouldn't have to stop and ask for directions. You can bet the ground crew got out of car-pool duty too.

----

[9]Available from the Sharper Image catalog in four designer colors (gray, gunmetal gray, battleship gray and Dorian Gray) and three styles (colonial, contemporary and Michael Jackson).

[10]A country not known for playing host to balloonists, especially one who bore such a striking resemblance to General Norman Schwarzkopf.

The French Have a Word for It

But are we wrong about what drives middle-aged men to such derring-do and derring-don't? It must take more than a desire to shirk responsibility to motivate someone who gets winded chalking up a pool cue to suddenly start training for the Tour de France. The answer is simple: They're out of their minds.

Luckily, there is a medical term for this condition (but don't bet on it being covered by your HMO). As usual, the Europeans were the first to recognize and name it: *andropause*. The French in particular like to write tedious journal articles on the subject, akin to their exhaustive study of the films of Jerry Lewis, while the Swedes explore the phenomenon in darkly lit films starring Max von Sydow as The Spectre of Death. Even the Canadians are way ahead of us on this one.

You ask, if women go through menopause, why don't men go through "womenopause"? Good question, even if you didn't ask it. Women at midlife take on male characteristics: they cannot bear children, they sprout facial hair and they sweat a lot—thus, "*men*opause."[11] Men, of course, do not become like women as they age; they become even more *andro*—"manlike": highly irritable, too fatigued to help with the housework and obsessed with sex.

Yet, ironically, this coincides with the andropausal man's diminishing sexual performance. For this reason, the term "viropause"[12] was coined by the British, who, at the time, were trying to recover from Prince Charles cooing to his liver-spotted lover, Camilla Parker-Bowles, "I want to live in your trousers"[13] and suggesting that he wanted to be reincarnated as her

---

[11]No, no, I'm only kidding, of course. *Menopause* derives from the cessation of the menses, or menstrual cycle, while *mensapause* means that *Parade Magazine* columnist Marilyn vos Savant is on vacation.

[12]Throughout this book, I will use the terms andropause, viropause and male menopause interchangeably, so I won't have to keep track of which term I used last.

[13]This only seems silly if you don't know that, like saying "lift" for "elevator," the Brits use the term "trousers" to mean "pants."

tampon.[14] *Viropause,* though, implies that this stage is merely a pause in virility. The truth is, this is no Time Out, pal; it's Game Over. And that is what many men have difficulty accepting.

Overachieving American men, as well as the British musical group The Rolling Stones, seem to have the hardest time accepting that there is a biological limit to their machismo. Instead of addressing the decline of their physical and mental abilities, they feel they must test their limits and everyone else's patience. Subsequently, the andropausal man is often misunderstood by his doctors, significant other, ex-wife or the readers of *The National Star.*

No matter how many nebbishy filmmakers, nebbishy presidential campaign advisors, nebbishy S&L officers or nebbishy late-night talk-show hosts make the headlines because of sexual, political, financial or speed-limit indiscretions, no members of a national health task force have made the connection that this is a widespread problem with a biological, as well as a psychological, basis. Why not? Because most national health task forces are made up of middle-aged men who are fully occupied with their own sexual, political, financial or speed-limit indiscretions and are just trying to get out of car-pool duty.

IRON JOHN, MEET TUPPERWARE PHIL

At first I didn't know what was happening. I was drenched in a cold sweat and my heart was pounding harder than the drums I had beaten with Robert Bly. Since I'd just finished watching The Sports Illustrated Bathing Suit Calendar Video, *I didn't think much of it at the time. But that night the same symptoms woke me from a deep sleep and I heard myself screaming out loud: "Not yet! I've never gone bungee-jumping! I've never rafted down the Colorado! I've never had Claudia Schiffer!" I felt old, old, old.*

[14]The British spelling of "tax accountant."

That was Phil[15]—an unusually self-aware Teamster who has memorized parts of *Fire in the Belly,* gone in search of his Inner Warrior and once took a pastry-making class—describing his first "cold flash." In his 30s, Phil had learned about Iron John, the ancient hairy man in the Brothers Grimm fairy tale who helps a young boy through the stages of male growth. Phil had hoped that this myth would guide him through his own struggles with his manhood. Instead, the aging Phil has found that he is becoming less hairy—at least, in the places that count—and, brother, is he grim! Disillusioned, he stores his pain away in an airtight container deep within his refrigerated soul. But sometimes the lid cracks open just enough to let out a wrenching burp of emotion—thus, instead of transforming into Iron John, he has become Tupperware Phil.

Symptoms like his seem to surface around age 40, sometimes triggered by viewing a racy video, a *National Geographic* special on the desert people of the Serengeti or reruns of *American Gladiators.* About 5 percent of men may show signs of andropause earlier, say in their mid-to-late 30s, just so they can boast they got in on it before everyone else. Another 10 percent may wait until 60, when they can use their senior citizen's discount at the laser-tag course.

Dr. Aubrey Hill, an Oregon physician who dared to write a serious book called, redundantly, *Viropause/Andropause,* estimates that 15 out of 100 men have symptoms severe enough to require medical intervention. What he fails to mention is that another 15 have symptoms severe enough to require religious intervention. The rest require police intervention.

Your man, however, may not seek out such help, simply because he does not realize the complexity of his problem. All he knows is that he has followed a career path he did not choose, that his youthful dreams are no longer attainable and that if he had not married so young, he could be dating a

---

[15]Actually, Phil is a composite of several different men, all of whom, surprisingly, are named Phil.

supermodel. The bottom line: Whatever he's doing, wherever he is, whomever he is with—well, it's just not what he really had in mind. And it's all his mother's fault.

In addition, he may manifest some vague physical symptoms. He may complain of feeling "out of sorts," "breathless" or "a crushing pain in my chest." He may seem genuinely puzzled by the changes in his body: "Why does my left arm feel numb?" When you answer, "Because you're having a heart attack," he seems unwilling to accept your diagnosis and even more unwilling to get into the ambulance.

Not that an angioplasty alone would relieve his symptoms. Until recently, American doctors have shrugged off their middle-aged male patients' irrational behavior and physical complaints as the inevitable signs of "aging," a "midlife crisis" or an "inoperable brain tumor." Luckily, recent research—showing that the men most affected by andropause fall into a higher income bracket—has convinced physicians that there's big money in it, and they're taking the condition much more seriously.

Before now, andropausal men have had to look for other ways to deal with their feelings of discontent and anxiety. This led first to the invention of beer, then Foosball. (In combination, this still temporarily relieves symptoms for many men.) Others could only feel good about themselves by oppressing others, so they joined the Ku Klux Klan or the priesthood. When both of these fraternal organizations started getting unfavorable publicity, some members ran for Congress. Other men created the so-called men's movement, which shifted some blame from mothers and placed it squarely on fathers now too feeble to take their whiny sons out to the woodshed for a good whuppin'. The bonus was that it gave these existentially disoriented men another night out with the boys. At ever-growing gatherings, they were told to rediscover their Wild Man and their Inner Child—which, for most, was a simple matter of looking in the bathroom mirror. Predictably, the attendance at these gatherings dwindled when it came each man's turn to bring the refreshments.

THE UNFORGIVEN

But give our guys credit. Male baby boomers are the first generation to at least try to get in touch with their feminine side—or, in a pinch, someone else's feminine side. When he was younger, your man struggled with how to abandon his traditional male role without looking like a wuss. He even changed his kids' diapers, once he discovered pull-on disposables. Now that he's facing his Final Frontier, however, he's wondering if his time would have been better spent as a soldier of fortune.

The transition to midlife may be harder for these groundbreaking men. Because they had higher goals, they found it more difficult to get over them without pulling a hamstring. More tragically, if they had aimed too low, they left little driblets all over the floor for you to clean up.

Today's andropausal man has no role model for this later stage of life. Oh, sure, he watched his own father growing old, but the modern man does not see himself wearing a cardigan sweater, rubbing on Ben-Gay and reminiscing about "the good old days." Instead, he dons a Harley-Davidson jacket, rubs on Oil of Olay and reminisces about *Happy Days*.

He is validated by Hollywood, where time stands still. Older actors—so close to death that their whole-life insurance premiums have skyrocketed—are cast as action heroes. (Meanwhile, actresses who have barely turned 35 play mothers with grown-up children.)[16] Ever since the geriatric Charles Bronson starred in *Death Wish* several decades ago, the top box-office draws of recent years have been andropausal he-men: Mr. Universe (Senior Division), Arnold Schwarzenegger; bifocal-wearing Sylvester Stallone; Rogaine reject Bruce Willis; and Centrum Silver–medal winner Clint Eastwood. After a day

---

[16]Best example: then-37-year-old Angela Lansbury brainwashing her 34-year-old "son" Laurence Harvey in *The Manchurian Candidate*. Or more recently, then-48-year-old Sally Field mothering then-38-year-old Tom Hanks in *Forrest Gump*. Stupid is as stupid does.

leaping over parked cars, each of these tough guys retires to his movie-set trailer, where a sweet young thing probably helps him into his cardigan sweater, rubs him with Ben-Gay and reminisces about the Mike Ovitz years.

Defying—thus denying—their own aging bodies, then, becomes the new goal of some andropausal men. They take up physical challenges they wouldn't have considered only a few years ago. If they were paid $12 million and a percentage of the action-toy sales, it might make sense to jump off a railroad bridge with a giant rubber band around their ankles. But these guys do it for nothing and they could get hurt—especially after their wives find out what they're up to.

ATTORNEYS ON ICE, BUTCHERS IN THE OPERATING ROOM

After his 40th birthday, Mark declared that he would hike a local mountain range—all 48 peaks. That winter, to condition himself for camping in subzero temperatures, he sculpted an ice cave from the snow in his backyard. Every night for a week, he entered his cave to sleep; every morning, he emerged to return to his house, rub noses with his bewildered family and ready himself for work. Only the legal hassle and a cholesterol problem prevented him from changing his name to Nanook and eating whale blubber.[17] His clients drove by, proudly pointing him out: "That's my lawyer in that igloo."

As an attorney, Mark had to confine his mountaineering to the weekends (the judicial system has rather strict rules about lawyers actually showing up in court, especially if their clients have been deemed a flight risk). Each Saturday and Sunday he would set out with hope, determination and a backpack full of freeze-dried tofu. More than a year and a half later, he reached the summit of his last summit, where he forewent his usual Soy Cheese Saint Jacques and feasted on

---

[17]Tastes just like chicken blubber.

smoked salmon.[18] He returned home to share his triumph (but not his salmon) with his still-bewildered family. Unfortunately, he failed to recognize them: one of his two teenage daughters had shaved her head as smooth as a polar ice cap; the other had dyed her hair to resemble a Hudson's Bay blanket. But this did not lessen his sense of accomplishment. He relives his experience every time he hangs by his chin from the at-home traction device[19] he had to install in his kitchen to relieve the back pain that developed from sleeping in ice caves and carrying too much tofu.

Others have no time for such frivolous pursuits—so they *make* time, often by giving up the careers they spent two decades building. For instance, the CEO of a multinational company in Oregon shifted gears to open his own bicycle shop. Sadly, his skill at derailing corporate takeovers did not translate well into derailleurs, and he was soon on the skids. He tried to return to his old job, but had injured his back[20] pedaling too hard to keep up. By the time he got off disability, he had been unseated at work. Still, he learned something from the downsizing: He now downsizes horse stables—building miniature models (presumably, for miniature horses) that he sells at tack shops.

Not all midlife career changes are so dramatic. Some men discover that they can adapt their previous skills to a similar but more soul-satisfying line of work. My distant cousin Jim can still use many of his old tools in his new job; a successful butcher for 25 years, he's now a surgeon. After one of his two sons finished medical school, Jim decided to pursue his own dream. He knew that he wanted to help others and perhaps get into a real rowdy fraternity. So he went off in search of higher education—in his case, high school, which he had forgotten to graduate. Eventually he finished college, too,

---

[18]Available from the Eddie Bauer catalog for $26 a pound. Available in Jewish delis as "lox" for $7.95.

[19]No longer available through the Sharper Image catalog.

[20]The back seems to be the andropausal man's Achilles heel. Hey, great Christmas gift idea: a truss.

and was surprised to discover that no medical school in the
United States wanted someone with an AARP membership.
So Jim went off to Mexico, where meat cleavers are stan-
dard-issue surgical equipment. The World's Oldest Medical
Intern at 62, he went into partnership with his son the doctor. The last I heard, they were being sued for malpractice by
another, soon-to-be-distant cousin. Good thing Jim had sent
his other son to law school.

Some andropausal men do go a little overboard—changing careers, wives and/or states without leaving a forward-
ing address. After his wife left him, an executive of a utilities
company shortcircuited his job to take sailing lessons. Once
he was reasonably sure he knew his mast from his elbow, he
bought his own 25-foot sailboat and caught the next steady
breeze from Connecticut to Key West, with his new girlfriend
as his first mate. Once in Florida, and probably still disoriented from the ocean voyage, he married her. For the honeymoon, they and the sailboat headed to Montana (not a
state known for its regattas). He should have fired his travel
agent; instead he set fire to the sailboat. For some inexplica-
ble reason, his new wife divorced him soon after. The moral:
Once burned, twice ridiculous.

But perhaps the most extreme reaction to aging is exhibited
by men who go through viropause *and* menopause. I'm talking
about transvestites. Some zany Canadian researchers studied a
group of them in a gender identity clinic[21] and were just fasci-
nated. Twenty-one of these men, ages 40 to 65 years, suddenly
put aside their copies of *Vogue* and requested "surgical sex reas-
signment"—which sounds like just a little extra paperwork, but
in reality can be very painful and almost certainly irreversible.
This surprised the researchers, who knew from reading Ann
Landers' column that transvestites are usually heterosexual,
albeit with an unusual interest in the spring fashion collec-
tions. Even more shocking to the easily shocked Canadians

---

[21]Also probably not covered by your HMO.

was that the transvestites who wanted to alter their "outie" to an "innie" were the most macho of the group. The researchers concluded that this desire to "become a woman" was a defense mechanism masking midlife depression. Other researchers concluded that the desire to "become a man" was a defense mechanism masking Richard Simmons.

What is the point of these true-life stories? Be glad you are not married to any of these men. And if you were, that would be bigamy.

The Andropausal Man in the Media

Periodicals, films and literature are filled with clues to understanding your andropausal man. You might want to check out the following resources.

Magazines That Will Help You Understand Your Andropausal Man

Men's Journal
Motor Trend's Performance Cars
Iron Man
Islands
Child

Movies That Will Help You Understand Your Andropausal Man[22]

CARNAL KNOWLEDGE (1971) Two self-centered young men develop into two self-centered middle-aged men, leaving moviegoers wondering, "Why did Art Garfunkel break up with Paul Simon?" Jack Nicholson plays himself.

---

[22]Note: Contrary to popular movie reviews, *City Slickers* is *not* a male menopause movie, because parts of it were funny and it had a sequel.

LAST TANGO IN PARIS (1973) After his wife commits suicide, Marlon Brando has a kinky three-day affair with an engaged woman young enough to be his nutritionist. The movie has a happy ending, when she shoots him in the stomach. (Biographical note: In real life, French actress Maria Schneider later had a nervous breakdown, possibly when she learned that Brando was paid $3 million for 3 days' work in *Superman* despite having blown up to the size of the planet Krypton.)

THAT CHAMPIONSHIP SEASON (1982) Five hometown friends meet to reminisce about their days on a winning basketball team 25 years ago. Three of them—Bruce Dern, Paul Sorvino and Martin Sheen—try to come to grips with the realization that their children are now bigger movie stars than they ever were. They wonder if their kids will lend them money.

THAT'S LIFE! (1986) Architect Jack Lemmon wakes up on his 60th birthday to discover that he's married to Julie Andrews. The shock sets him on a self-destructive course of *Grumpy Old Men* movies, in which he co-stars with an oversized basset hound—oh, sorry, that's Walter Matthau.

EVERY CLINT EASTWOOD MOVIE EVER MADE A lone gunslinger/policeman/Secret Service agent rides into town, shoots everyone, serves justice and never says a word. This is who your andropausal man really believes he is deep down inside, except for the part about riding into town, shooting everyone and serving justice.

Books That Will Not Help You Understand Your Andropausal Man Because They Were Written by Andropausal Men in Denial

Iron John, by Robert Bly
Fire in the Belly, by Sam Keen
Men Are From Mars, Women Are From Venus, by John Gray
The Celestine Prophecy, by James Redfield
Anything by Robert James Waller

JUST THE F.A.Q.S, MA'AM

Q. *If there really is, as you say, such a thing as male menopause, why hasn't the public been informed?*

A. *The Journal of the American Medical Association* printed findings on the subject as early as 1939. World War II broke out the next day. Coincidence?

Q. *Why has so little research been done on viropause?*

A. Research of any nature involves at least four Ph.D.s, usually male. It takes, on average, 31 years to become a Ph.D. Ph.D.s cannot get a job in the outside world, so they must be employed by universities—usually sporadically. They will bounce around from university to university until they get tenure, submitting grant applications as they go. Their applications will be rejected many, many times. So it could take an additional 10 years before they can even think of ordering the necessary spider monkeys.[23] By the time the funding and personnel are in place, the Ph.D.s are in the throes of viropause themselves and have resigned their posts to become park rangers.

Q. *How can I tell whether my man is going through andropause or he's just eaten a bad piece of fish?*

A. Bad fish has an ammonia-like odor.

Q. *How long does andropause last?*

A. How much time does he have?

Q. *Is andropause fatal?*

A. Only if his symptoms become very advanced and you have a gun.

[23]Genetically a perfect match for viropausal men.

Q. *My middle-aged man keeps bringing home fishnet outfits he bought "for me" at Victoria's Secret, implying that I need some help getting aroused. I think he's the one with the problem, so shouldn't he be dressing up in a G-string and WonderBra?*

A. First of all, let me have a moment to get that unappealing image out of my mind.

Okay, that's better. Now, you mustn't take these purchases as a criticism of your own sex appeal, even though your first two thoughts may be:

1. I will look like Moby-Dick caught in a seining net.

2. I will have to shave. Everything.

At this time of his life, he needs more visual stimulation to pump his stump, but his ego is too frail to accept that idea. So accept the gift graciously and consider this his way of making an offering to his love goddess. Or as one man explained it more romantically, "It's like giving a good set of golf clubs to a really good golfer." (Surprisingly, this statement is not sufficient grounds for divorce in 26 states.) Then put it on for him, knowing full well that it will not fit since he's never bought you so much as lip gloss in the right size. Then sweetly whisper to him Victoria's real secret: Underwear is nonreturnable. That will really get him aroused.

By the way, here's another helpful hint: with a little hot soapy water and some elbow grease, fishnet will remove scorched-on food from your old baking pans.

Q. *It sounds like you have some unresolved issues in this area. Is everything okay at home?*

A. I don't want to talk about it.

Q. *Why are all the detectives on TV and in the movies portrayed by middle-aged men? My husband can't detect a gallon of milk in the refrigerator.*

A. The problem, of course, is that the entertainment media is controlled by middle-aged men—men who were once teenagers who spent a lot of time alone, reading *X-Men* comic books and playing with their Dad's Super 8 home-movie camera. Now that they are adults, they can create worlds where they are the heroes who do not have to clean up their rooms. A typical scenario: The hard-working movie male comes back from an exhausting day performing open-heart surgery, investigating a grisly serial murder committed by John Malkovich or Kevin Spacey, or saving the world from alien beings who look like the doe-eyed figures in a "Love Is" cartoon, and all he wants to do is relax and talk about his *feelings*. The woman always responds, "Well, I know how I can fix *that*," then she straddles him and starts unbuttoning his shirt or her shirt or both. In fact, this fantasy is taking place in your teenage son's bedroom right now, so go knock on the door and tell him to finish his homework so he can graduate high school and become Steven Spielberg.

But I digress. From a purely physiological viewpoint, as men age and lose muscle strength, they become incapable of moving aside the orange juice carton, which is always conspiring with the water jug to block his view of the dairy products.

Q. *After chopping garlic, how do I remove the smell from my hands?*

A. You want *The Best of "Hints From Heloise."* Try the next aisle.

2

Men: The Awkward Years
(Birth to Death)

You can think of maleness as a type of birth defect.
—Dr. Stephen Wachtel, perinatal pathologist,
as quoted in *Love, Sex, Death and the Making of the Male,*
by Rosalind Miles

*A*s men and women age, so do their hormones. In menopausal women, estrogen levels drop so severely that they are reported to resemble the Space Mountain ride at Disney World.[24] Andropausal men, however, suffer a *slow* leak of testosterone, which they are always meaning to have fixed but never get around to, because . . . well, they're just too busy. The manifestations of this gradual hormonal ebbing can be frightening to men who have given little thought to the possibility of losing their virility. In other words, to ALL men. Mood swings, self-doubt, irritability, insensitivity—while evident in males from birth—become so extreme they're even noticeable to the men themselves. Some would say (well, women would say) andropause is difficult to distinguish from everyday male behavior.

To really understand the changes at viropause, then, we must look at how men are affected by the rise and fall of testosterone throughout their lives. But first, let's step

---

[24]Mouse, Minnie, *Look Out, Mickey! Here Comes Another One!: 101 Hot Flashes* (Hyperion Books, 1993).

farther back and take a look at the hormone's evolution. Wait
. . . you've stepped too far back. That's better. Now, move a
little to your right. Okay, those of you in front, squat down a
little so the rest of us can see. Fine. Now we can begin:

Born to Be Wild

When dealing with men of any age, it all comes down to testosterone. Decades of biological research and scientific trials
prove without a doubt that this happy little hormone's effects
on the male persona program him for little more than pro-
creation, smashing beer cans against his forehead and hunting
giraffes.[25]

The word *testosterone* comes from the Middle English word
testy ("irritable"), the appliance name *Oster* ("blender") and
the Italian suffix *one* ("huge"). Which means that men are
"big, easily annoyed food processors." No, no, of course
that's not true—or, rather, the etymology is not true. *Testosterone* comes from *testis,* a Latin word meaning "witness" (as
in "Witness this huge pepperoni, *bambina,*" believed to have
been first uttered by a gladiator outside the Roman baths)
and *sterone,* the Japanese word for *Stallone.*

Testosterone starts as *androstenedione,* an immature and
indecisive hormone produced in the mother's ovaries. It has to
make up its mind in the placenta within seven weeks after con-
ception whether to become frilly estrogen or well-muscled
testosterone. Until this decision is made, everyone starts out
female, including J. Edgar Hoover. Unconsciously, men—having had to make such an earth-shattering choice so early in
life—are later reluctant to commit to anything more meaningful
than a tee-off time.

---

[25]Contrary to what Newt Gingrich tells us, men have little opportunity these
days to hunt giraffes—except in zoos, where the practice is discouraged.
However, this primitive biological urge has adapted to our industrial society:
men now assume that any driver who raises his middle finger at him on the
highway is a giraffe in disguise and should be hunted down and killed.

The pair of sex chromosomes that we all inherit with our DNA helps nudge the decision along. A female-to-be gets two big healthy X chromosomes, while a male winds up with a sturdy X and a puny, mutation-prone Y chromosome, which is responsible for questions like:

"Y can't I take my carburetor apart on the dining-room table that's been in your family for six generations? It's old anyway."

"Y do we have to invite your parents to our daughter's college graduation? We just saw them at our wedding 30 years ago."

"Y are you leaving me?"

Anyway, somewhere around that seventh week, the male-apparent embryo awaits word from a single gene on the Y chromosome.[26] Like Punxsutawney Phil, the groundhog harbinger of spring, this gene may or may not come out of hibernation and see its shadow. If it does, it stimulates the embryo's undeveloped gonads into producing testosterone, ensuring six more months of nuclear winter. If it doesn't, the embryo becomes distinctly feminine and looks forward to 18 years of humiliation in gym class.

The testosterone released by the tiny testes wakes up the brain to start constructing a penis and scrotum from the female parts.[27] Along with the extra and endlessly fascinating apparatus they get in this process, males also gain a propensity toward color blindness, dyslexia, hemophilia, high blood pressure and homophobia. It is believed that excess exposure to testosterone before birth may be responsible for left-handedness and an interest in professional wrestling.[28] A toxic level of testosterone produces the National Football League; a low level produces florists.

---

[26]Discovered recently by the British, this gene, viewed under incredibly high magnification, closely resembles comedian Benny Hill.

[27]Researchers have conducted many complex studies to show what happens when the ovaries of a newborn female mouse are implanted into a newborn male mouse, but all of them should be reported to the ASPCA.

[28]Interestingly, a male gerbil flanked in the womb by two brothers gets hit with extra testosterone from two sides and is born bigger, heavier and smellier than his siblings. Worse, he hogs time on the play wheel and won't share his Purina Gerbil Chow.

Once this early testosterone is finished constructing the male additions, it grabs a brewski and goes to sleep. For about 12 years.

Fire in the Belly—Where's the Mylanta?

Just as all feminine traits are known by the initials *PMS*, any stereotypically masculine behavior can be summed up by the word *testosterone*. And research confirms that this hormone *is* responsible for many of the physical and personality traits of maleness—not just his Mighty Morphin' Power Ranger (or whatever pet name your man has given his genitals), but also how he reasons, behaves at buffets and finds his car in a crowded stadium parking lot. More alarming, testosterone speeds up his brain's development and solidifies any early programming *while still in the womb*. In essence, a male's brain, dipped as it is in testosterone, becomes inflexible, even before his baby shoes are bronzed. *Now* do you see why you can never get him to change his mind more than 40 years later?

Testosterone's early influence on behavior has been well documented in mammal studies. For instance, male *and* female hyenas are heavily drenched in testosterone in the mother's womb, and the aggressiveness of both sexes is legendary: "In less than 30 minutes, a group of two dozen hyenas can reduce a 500-pound adult zebra to a blood stain on the ground," animal behaviorist Dr. Laurence ("All Meat"?) Frank cheerily told the *New York Times*. (In humans, the same phenomenon has been observed in a group of volunteer firemen on All-You-Can-Eat Rib Night at the Sizzler.) Hyena babies, usually born in pairs, emerge directly from the womb with their eyes open, muscles tensed and teeth bared, ripping at each other's throats until one of them is dead. Now let's see the Nature Channel make something cute out of *that*.

Yet some scientists question whether testosterone itself is at the root of such violence; they've found that men with *low* testosterone levels report feeling angry and out of sorts until they're given as much as all their friends have. Others have noted a connection between aggression and men with very low cholesterol; soon murder suspects will be using the *Dr. Dean Ornish's Program for Reversing Heart Disease* defense. But that *would* be justifiable homicide. Anyone who follows Ornish's inhumanely low-fat diet would be so irritable he could easily rip apart a hyena with his bare hands.

GUNS: A BOY'S BEST FRIEND

For the ultimate proof that aggression is innately male, though, stop at any nursery school. Almost as soon as they can close their little hands into a fist, boys release their index finger, cock back their thumbs and start firing. PATTOO-PATTOO issues forth from their tiny, milk-stained lips— those same little lips that had only recently suckled at your breast, before his teeth started coming in. And this is during the time testosterone is supposed to be *napping*.

OBJECTS LITTLE BOYS PRETEND ARE GUNS

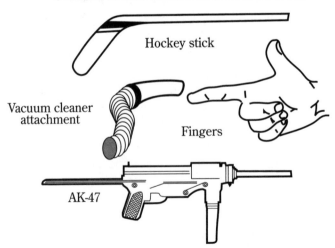

Hockey stick

Vacuum cleaner attachment

Fingers

AK-47

The male's attraction to guns, bombs, bazookas, torpedoes and other cylindrical shapes packed with explosive power seems to be instinctual. But how do little boys make the connection between their penises and weapons and not between, say, their penises and bratwurst? Maybe former Surgeon General Jocelyn Elders was right. If masturbation or German sausage-making were taught in the schools, most of the major world wars and not a few post-office massacres could have been avoided.

IS THAT A SUBPOENA IN YOUR POCKET OR ARE YOU JUST HAPPY TO SEE ME?

The majority of data does seem to show that testosterone is linked to competitiveness—which pretty much confirms that the need to dominate is a "man thing," unless, of course, you're Madonna. How much testosterone your man winds up with at birth may also influence his career choices later in life.

Dr. James ("Jimmy Dribble"?) Dabbs, a researcher at Georgia State University, measures saliva for a living. No, not just for fun, but because there's testosterone in it. Not surprisingly, Dr. Dabbs discovered that ministers were low on the testosterone scale. More interestingly, men with higher-than-normal levels of testosterone tend to become trial lawyers or criminals. Of course, that opens up other questions, such as: Who can tell them apart? Can they represent themselves in court? And, more importantly, what does Mrs. Dr. Dabbs do when she finds her husband's drool-covered lab coats tossed on their bedroom floor? Does she use a prewash?

So, what makes a high-test guy decide between earning his living through armed robbery or from, say, defending an ex-football player who is obviously a murderer? Evidence suggests that the social or economic class they are born into determines how they channel their domineering personalities. Another factor is whether or not they own a ski mask.

TURN RIGHT AT THE NEXT VECTOR

While champions of Constitutional rights would like us to believe that the sexes are equal, this is nonsense to any wife who has returned home after a two-day business trip to find every utensil and all the Corningware sitting in the sink, encrusted with food.[29] To get back at feminists, some scientists have been studying how sex hormones affect brain structures, to prove that men process information differently from women, if at all.

For instance, because of their hormones, males can look at drawings of three-dimensional objects and mentally "rotate" them to "see" the drawings at different angles. When they get tired of that, they pick up a Rubik's Cube and waste a few more hours.[30] This spatial reasoning also gives males the upper hand in mathematics, reading maps, picking out a figure hidden in a complex background and throwing or catching a ball—cognitive skills that women couldn't care less about even if they were good at them. On the downside, men are less adept at reading emotions on a human face, even when the mouth on that face has said several times, very loudly, "I'm so furious I could kill you."

Testosterone also gets a man where he is today—going around and around in circles. Dr. Thomas ("Eager"?) Bever, a professor at the University of Rochester, reported during a Quebec symposium that men follow a navigating system that relies on a primitive sense of motion using remembered vectors, such as direction, time and speed. Women, on the other hand, find their way by noting landmarks. Neither method of navigation is superior, insists Dr. Bever, who is a man. But this may explain why your husband won't stop and ask for

---

[29]Note that men invented the dishwasher but still haven't figured out how to empty it.

[30] Interestingly, women do 50 to 100 percent better on the mental-rotation test during their menstrual cycle, when estrogen levels are lowest. But they are still not bored enough to pick up a Rubik's Cube.

directions, particularly when driving to the home of one of *your* relatives. Even though *you* know he's lost, he doesn't *feel* lost—he thinks he's just misplaced his vectors. Now, if he can only remember what vectors are.

> WIFE [*following her primitive instincts*]: Just go down Main Street to Gundersen's, where I bought those slingbacks at 50 percent off. Make a right. Then go past the Buns of Cinnamon bakery and make a left at Baskin & Jerry's 1,072 Flavors and . . .
> HUSBAND [*following his primitive instincts*]. What are you talking about? I have to proceed north-by-northwest for 38 minutes at 63 miles per hour, make a 98.6-degree left turn and then a sharp right, and then . . . [*sound of splashing*]
> WIFE: Tom, you just drove into a lake. And I don't think this is Rochester.

In a related experiment, Dr. Christina Williams of Barnard College discovered that male rats became lost when the shape of the room outside their maze was changed, whereas female rats became confused when large objects in the room were moved around at random. This shatters all assumptions that women's compulsion to rearrange furniture is a purely hostile gesture to men. Women are just hoping they won't be able to find their own way back to the kitchen.

In a fit of jealousy, Dr. Bever created his own test, asking men and women to identify, and arrange in sequence, photographs of intersections in his university's underground tunnel system. The women, of course, did better, as they were able to note subtle differences in the photos. "Frankly, *I* couldn't make head nor tail of them," Dr. Bever confessed to the *New York Times*. Unfortunately, Dr. Bever could not be reached for further comment; he hasn't yet found his way back from the symposium, held in May 1992.

The final question still not answered by this research: If men are so good at reading maps, why don't they use them? But perhaps that serves an evolutionary purpose as well. If Christopher Columbus had consulted his AAA Triptiks to find his way to the Indies, today the Native American casinos would be empty.

TO EVERY THINGAMAJIG THERE IS A SEASON

As every woman and every politician who wants to keep women out of military combat knows, estrogen follows a monthly cycle. But testosterone is even more erratic: it fluctuates with the seasons. The University of Western Ontario's Dr. Doreen Kimura, another of those research-crazy Canadians, found that testosterone is lowest in the spring and highest in autumn, explaining why the World Series drags on until October. On the plus side, the low testosterone levels of spring seem to improve a man's mathematical ability— around April, which is why he must put off filing your tax return until the last minute.

Testosterone also goes through a *daily* change. Levels are highest in the morning, around 4 A.M., dipping down during the day to their lowest point at 8 P.M. He has a slight, sudden surge later on in the evening—roughly at the time he suspects you've fallen into a deep sleep—and wants to wake you to tell you about it.

Obviously, these hormonal shifts mean men are unstable for most of the typical workday and from Thanksgiving until the following Labor Day. Proof enough, along with Pat Robertson, that men should be kept from pursuing high posts in government.

EVERYTHING HE NEEDS TO KNOW
HE LEARNED IN JUNIOR HIGH

Where were we? Oh, yes. Around age 12, testosterone wakes up and starts to get surly and wants its own way all the time. Think of it: suddenly, a boy has *18 times* the amount of testosterone pumping through his system, and *2 million times* the body hair. That would be enough to make anyone's voice crack.

Testosterone stimulates such changes, called secondary sex characteristics, in one form or other in all males of the animal world. In a classic study, scientists injected capons with extra testosterone and watched as the birds' combs grew larger and larger. (Why a group of grown researchers would find this amusing requires another study.) And who but the male authors of a human physiology textbook would proudly claim that testosterone is responsible for the "deep attracting voice of the tree toad"?

> MALE TREE TOAD [*in a deep attracting voice*]: What's your sign? Ribbet! [*unfurls his tongue to snag a gnat*]
> FEMALE TREE TOAD [*gives him a withering look and slides off her toadstool, vowing never to come to one of these singles' lily pads ever again*].

Upon puberty, male salamanders know how to perform an exotic courtship dance that, sadly, has no counterpart in male human behavior, though I'd pay good money to see it. But without having to try very hard, an adolescent boy does gain bigger muscles and a much, much bigger . . . other muscle.

That's when he knows it's time to rename his pee-wee.[31] Elvis Presley named his, not very originally, "Little Elvis"; Lyndon Johnson liked to call his johnson "Jumbo." Robin Williams

---

[31]That's the name his mother gave it—*not* a self-esteem builder and probably the real reason he never calls her on her birthday.

delightfully addresses his significant other as "Mr. Happy." A few other options: The Terminator, Apollo 13, Mr. Deeds.[32]

It's only fitting that men should give this distinct part of their anatomy its own name. They really believe it *is* another guy whispering, "Oh, go on! Who's it gonna hurt?" Testosterone is responsible for men's all-powerful urge to merge,[33] making sex uppermost in his mind for the rest of his life, or until his mind is removed for organ donation (see diagram, below). The push to procreate is so overwhelming that, in an as-yet-unconducted experiment, it was proven that if a man had his arm caught in a wood chipper and a woman approached him to suggest a sexual liaison, he would reply, "Let me just get a Band-Aid for this and I'll be right with you."

THE MALE BRAIN

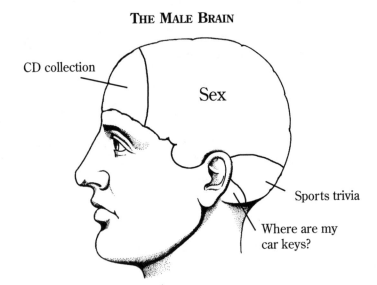

CD collection

Sex

Sports trivia

Where are my car keys?

---

[32]Nicknames that should warn you away: Gonad the Barbarian, The Space Needle, The Awful Tower, The International House of Pancakes, or Spot.
[33]Women also get their libido from testosterone, but they have about 10 times less of it, which is disappointing in terms of sex drive but does cut down on time spent with her Lady Schick.

But at 12, your baby-boomer man, a victim of the Ozzie-and-Harriet mentality of the '50s, wasn't quite sure what to do next. He couldn't talk to his parents about his feelings, because it never occurred to him that they might know anything about sex (if they did, they wouldn't have had that look on their faces). So he got his erotic education from the experts—*13*-year-old boys who heard it from 14-year-old boys. It's a primitive form of communication, like tribal drums or the childhood game of Telephone as played by Larry Flynt. The young boy also supplemented his lessons with extracurricular reading, such as *Playboy* and *National Geographic,* and educational films, such as *Barbarella* and *One Million Years B.C.,* and occasionally sneaking in the exit door of an adult-movie theater (remember—this was before cable!).

From these resources, young boys gleaned their entire understanding of human sexuality and, through their research, found that often sex didn't even have to involve a woman. As they grew older, involved a women, dated and married, they still looked to magazines, movies and TV to explain the facts of life:

> **1.** *Women are attracted by the smell of beer.* In fact, the sound of a pop-top opening is the mating call of the Swedish Bikini Ski Team.
> **2.** *Women prefer nerdy men.* They learned this from early Woody Allen movies and get continuing proof from later Woody Allen movies, *Wayne's World I* and *II* and any other movie starring an alumnus of *Saturday Night Live*.
> **3.** *Women have bladders of steel.* Even after having a few major organs batted around, they never need to excuse themselves before or during—kind of like camels, in reverse.
> **4.** *Women are highly absorbent.* They can do it in an elevator, on the kitchen table, in the backseat of a car and never need so much as a cocktail napkin afterward.

Of course, these perceptions set up your man for a lifetime of disappointment. When he finally got the chance to experience the real thing, he could not believe that this was all there was to it. He could only conclude that to re-create what he saw in still or moving pictures he would need a zeppelin-breasted woman without pores. Not once did any of his little friends explain the terms "retouched photograph," "plastic surgery" or "high divorce rate among supermodels."

Thereafter, no matter how many times his girlfriends or wives tried to explain the nature of female sexuality, he believed that these women were lying and that his childhood friend Kevin Reilly, whose sole medical skill at age 12 was exploratory surgery of his own nostrils and who is now serving 15 years for mail fraud, *really* knew how girls liked it.

We adolescent girls weren't any better informed. While the boys were exchanging foreplay advice ("two minutes— *tops*") under the elementary-school bleachers, the objects of their affection were watching a filmstrip of what they were told was their reproductive system but what was actually an aerial view of a Volkswagen Beetle trying to get past a school of gigantic guppies on the Los Angeles freeway at rush hour.

In high school, sex education involved explicit medical terms that would never find their way into a pickup line but would lead to the joke, "There's a *vas deferens* between men and women." Instead, teenagers should be taught phrases like, "Ow, you're leaning on my hair," "You need some help with that?" and "Could you roll over? My leg just fell asleep." (Note to policy makers: Taxpayer dollars would be much better spent showing adolescent boys and girls movies of real sex between real people—specifically, their parents. Teen pregnancy rates would plummet.)

How does this lead to an adolescent boy's lifelong obsession with electronic equipment? Beats me. Perhaps he assumes *woofers* and *tweeters* are slang terms for "breasts." He buys the biggest set he can afford. Once he has them plugged in, he becomes distracted with all the buttons and knobs, and he forgets why he wanted them. By accident he turns the volume way up and likes it; it makes his pee-wee vibrate. The sound waves bounce off the walls, turning his whole room into one of those hotel beds equipped with Magic Fingers. He thinks all that pulsating power will drive a woman wild. It does—but the woman is his mother.

The high decibel level of music in adolescence creates a phenomenon peculiar only to men: selective deafness. For some reason, he can no longer hear the words "now," "clean," "appointment," "renewal notice," "amount due" and "canceled." The condition is worsened when exposed to marriage.

THE ONE-EYED WORM

While testosterone does speed up sperm production, men do not realize that they should take especial pains to preserve their precious output. The reason: a recent study on—no coincidence here—worms showed that those who ejaculated more often had a shorter life span. In fact, those who were castrated lived 50 percent longer.[34] Can data from comma-sized worms be applied to human-sized males? Who cares? Assume that it does and bring it up in conversation as often as possible.

Many researchers are wondering why males are needed in the reproductive process at all. Considering how much of the female's time they take up and how little they're involved in child-rearing, these scientists figure Nature should have eliminated them by now. Other species have evolved into asexual females that get by just fine, taking out the garbage and doing all lawn maintenance themselves.

It also turns out that sperm is often defective; it's up to 100 times more likely than a female's egg to cause a genetic

---

[34]Not that this gives them a break on their life insurance premiums. These worms, on average, live only 14 days—versus 8.1 days if allowed to copulate like worms.

mutation that might result in a weak or diseased offspring. So males aren't even ensuring the survival of the species! One theory suggests that male-female intercourse accidentally began when one primordial organism[35] devoured the other to survive, sort of like Tom Arnold and Roseanne (though in their case, it's not clear who devoured whom). But unlike their marriage, these organisms' coupling proved to be good for that species and caught on. And now because of what happened more than 1.5 billion years ago between two consenting giant-kelp cells, the rest of us have to suffer.

But even Harvard-trained scientists can overlook the obvious: perhaps the reason for man's existence is that he can be easily talked into giving a back massage.

You Just Don't Understand . . . Hey! Are You Even *Listening* to me?

After puberty, a male's testosterone level may range from 250 to 1,250 nanograms per deciliter of blood, with an average of 900 (though he'll lie and say he's batting 1,000). He'll reach his highest level around age 30, when he thinks he still has a chance to make CEO in the next five years.

Somewhere between the ages of 48 and 70, say some hormonal specialists, levels start to decline as much as 30 to 40 percent. Other researchers insist that the aging male's testosterone loss is minimal, at least until he's in his 70s, and has no effect on him. Yeah, right. He knows when you've moved one of his 4 million cassettes, given away the jeans he hasn't worn since Cream broke up or used his razor to shave your underarms. He's *not* going to notice that some of his magic potion is missing or make a fuss about it? Give me a break.

But now another group of med-school graduates has discovered that, while total testosterone may not drop

---

[35]If you need further proof, consider that the anagram for *organism* is "in orgasm."

drastically, what nose-dives is *free* testosterone—the active part of the hormone. When it is young, it lifts weights and frequents peep shows, but in later life it cruises the bloodstream wearing spandex without getting picked up by the body, which has gotten too old and tired to play along. Free testosterone may decline by 50 percent (the other 50 percent may accept but will ask if it can bring a date). This decrease may trigger the behavior that, barely tolerated in a male in the first flush of puberty, seems completely intolerable when your man must begin scheduling regular colorectal exams.

THE WONDER YEARS: TESTOSTERONE LEVELS FROM AGE 0 TO 90

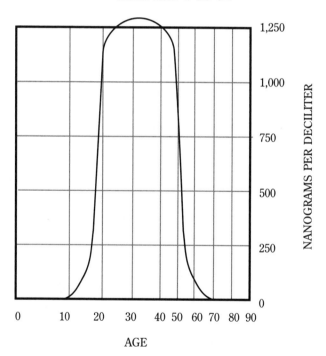

NANOGRAMS PER DECILITER

AGE

3

Men Are From Mars . . .
Women Just Wish They'd Remember to
Pick Up the Dry Cleaning on Their Way
Back to Earth

I don't believe in the male midlife crisis.
—Dr. John B. McKinlay, male epidemiologist,
as quoted in the *New York Times*

*P*erhaps you're not sure that your man is in the throes of andropause—or, more likely, *he* refuses to believe it. Sure, he thinks the CPA next door looks ridiculous in his metal-studded bomber jacket from The Squat Man's Annex at House of Leather, or that his brother-in-law has some nerve trying to pass off his infatuation with his new law clerk as a side effect of Agent Orange. But *him* a victim of male menopause?

Hey, don't take my word for it—I don't even know the guy. Really the only way to get an absolutely accurate diagnosis of his condition—and this is according to strict criteria set up by the American Medical Association—is to take a multiple-choice test in a book. Luckily, one follows.

You can try to guess his responses to the situations below, but it would be more fun to trick him into answering on his own. Tell him it's one of those *Cosmo* "How Sexy Is Your Mate?" quizzes. He's only half-listening anyway. Promise to give him a barbecue-flavored snack food if he cooperates.

IS HE LOSING IT? TEST HIS TESTOSTERONE

1. Noticing that his pants are starting to feel snug, he:
    a. restricts his food intake and engages in a thrice-
weekly program of aerobic exercise.   +0
    b. tightens his belt until his waistband slides
below his hips and his stomach folds over twice.   +1
    c. suggests that *you* go on a diet.   +2
BONUS POINTS if he buys you an AbMaster for
your birthday.   +3

2. He thoughtfully goes out to do some errands for
the family. Driving back from the supermarket, he:
    a. remembers to pick up the dry cleaning.   +0
    b. makes an obscene gesture at a station wagon full
of nuns who cut him off at an intersection.   +1
    c. trades in your minivan for a red Corvette.   +2
BONUS POINTS if he forgot to remove the groceries
and/or your toddler from the van's back seat.   +3

3. He's had a bad day at work, so he:
    a. comes home, opens up to you about his feelings
of frustration and kisses you tenderly.   +0
    b. comes home, opens the liquor cabinet and kisses
the dog.   +1
    c. leaves home, opens a Swiss bank account and
kisses off 25 years of marriage.   +2
BONUS POINTS if he takes the dog with him.   +3

4. He thinks his "look" needs updating, so he:
    a. buys a new pair of socks.   +0
    b. buys a new baseball cap and team jacket.   +1
    c. buys a wardrobe of silk tropical shirts, grows what's
left of his hair into a ponytail and pierces his nose.   +2
BONUS POINTS if he moves to Tahiti to paint
"real" women.   +3

5. As he passes a health club one morning on his way
to work, he notices a lovely young woman in leotards
coming out the door. He:

    a. thinks of how much she reminds him of you.   +0

    b. drools, whistles and/or makes animal noises.   +1

    c. goes to the office, calls you and asks for a trial
    separation.   +2

BONUS POINTS if he signs up for a 6 A.M. step-aerobics
class on the off-chance he'll see this young woman
again.   +3

6. He runs into an old rival from college who, he
discovers, now owns Utah and is married to a
former centerfold. He:

    a. smiles, shakes his rival's hand enthusiastically
    and says, "Congratulations!"   +0

    b. slightly exaggerates his own position in life—
    for example, mentions he's "in transportation"
    when, since the downsizing, he's been the cart
    boy at your local A&P.   +1

    c. runs into his rival again, this time with his car.   +2

BONUS POINTS if he then shifts into reverse.   +3

7. He's feeling a bit depressed, so he:

    a. rents a few Marx Brothers tapes from the
    video store.   +0

    b. tunes in to the "All Curly" Marathon on The
    Three Stooges Network.   +1

    c. gives up his senior vice presidency so he can
    hone his stand-up comedy act at Laughingstock's.   +2

BONUS POINTS if he travels the country performing at
open-mike nights.   +3

8. While at his barber's, he notices that his hair is
thinning, so he:

    a. vows to go bald with dignity and asks to have

the remaining strands trimmed stylishly.   +0
b. decides to switch barbers.   +1
c. starts crying, frantically examines his head from different angles in all the mirrors and has to be physically removed from the premises.   +2
BONUS POINTS if he takes to wearing a baseball cap to the office, in bed or while directing a $40-million motion picture.   +3

9. Because he's having a little trouble meeting your home-mortgage payments, he:
    a. draws up a carefully itemized budget, cancels his golf-club membership and plans on a stay-at-home vacation this year.   +0
    b. gets a cash advance on his MasterCard— because things are bound to get better once he closes The Big Deal.   +1
    c. buys a speedboat.   +2
BONUS POINTS if he also signs the lease on an oceanfront time-share.   +3

10. He pulled a groin muscle while playing shortstop for his company's softball team. Now that he's recovered, he:
    a. returns to the team, taking it slow.   +0
    b. treats himself to a month at fantasy baseball camp.   +1
    c. shows up in Tampa for spring tryouts.   +2
BONUS POINTS if he hires a professional pitching coach   +3

11. Afraid that he's losing touch with his almost-grown son, he:
    a. gives him a hug, tells him he loves him and let him know he's there for him if he ever needs his help.   +0

b. tosses a football around with him in the yard
for a while, then takes him out for a beer.   +1
c. talks to him about the importance of safe sex,
then asks him for the phone number of his
ex-girlfriend.   +2
BONUS POINTS if he drags his son and his nephew to
a singles bar on Easter Sunday and later has to
testify about it in court.   +3

12. He knows he has a good job, a loving family and
all the material comforts anyone could want. Yet he
would give them all up in a minute for:
  a. world peace.   +0
  b. a chance to replay his high school
  championship game.   +1
  c. a night with any of the *Baywatch* babes.   +2
BONUS POINTS If he *really* believes that he even has
a chance with Yasmine Bleeth.   +3

Now give him the snack and the sports section and
tally his score.

SCORING KEY
  0–11   *He's lying.*
  12–23   *He's a regular guy.*
  24–35   *He's a testosterone time bomb.*
  36–60   *He's the poster boy for andropause.*

Sadly, this quiz points out behavior manifested in the
advanced stages of andropause. Even if your man's score
indicates that he, and you, are not yet in danger, you should
be alert to some of the more subtle signs and symptoms. (Of
course, since they're subtle, he'll never notice them, so it's
up to you to let him know just how very far gone he is.)

THE 10 WARNING SIGNS OF ANDROPAUSE

1. OBSESSION WITH SEX

You know that during menopause a woman often experiences *formication* (the sensation of insects crawling all over her skin). Well, the andropausal man often experiences *fornication* (the sensation of someone else crawling all over his skin). Researchers have yet to determine a biological cause for this phenomenon, and most can hardly wait to experience it themselves.

It's obvious the basis is primarily psychological. The middle-aged man's unconscious registers that his testosterone is drip, drip, dripping away. His male ego is loathe to part with it—or with those junior-varsity bowling trophies that have been collecting dust in the attic and that you're gonna put curbside for the next trash pickup if he doesn't sort through his junk like he said he was going to last spring. For your man, then, sex becomes a preoccupation—not as it was in his younger years, when arousal was like a new router he couldn't wait to try out on different grades of lumber. No, it's rather like the chainsaw he lent your neighbor last summer—he longs desperately to get back what's rightfully his even if it means losing a longtime friendship.

Considering the tremendous role testosterone plays in sculpting the male personality, it's natural that he would feel threatened by the loss of even a nanogram of this precious life force. He feels he must devote all of his remaining energies toward regaining his youthful indulgence in frequent sex with virtual strangers or HE WILL CEASE TO BE. It will seem perfectly rational to him, and he will feel that anyone who tries to convince him otherwise—like you, his wife—should stand trial for manslaughter.

2. LOSS OF DESIRE

This may seem a contradiction in light of the viropausal man's heightened obsession with sex. However, it's obvious, if you've been paying attention, that it's just this lagging of his libido, due to the drop in his testosterone levels, that causes panic and overcompensation. He remembers when he was 14 years old and the mere suggestion of sex was stimulating; he could get turned on by Bugs Bunny in drag. Now not even Jessica Rabbit does it for him. His fragile ego cannot allow him to truly face his fear of flaccidity. So naturally he's sure it's all his wife's fault. To prove his theory and ensure a successful sexual performance, he may seek out females who could not fail but excite any man whose EKG is not a flat line.

For a time, the attentions of a nubile supermarket cashier may give him the illusion of potency, even though he still falls asleep at the first strains of the *Nightline* theme music. But that won't last for long, as his young lover will eventually run off with the store's produce manager. It may even take the andropausal man a few weeks to notice she's gone. Still convinced the problem lies with his partner, he will find another dewy-eyed young woman—perhaps one who doesn't speak fluent English or is just finishing up junior high. Thus begins a vicious cycle.

3. HAIR LOSS/GAIN

Male-pattern baldness is considered a consequence of genetics, a trait inherited from the maternal side. Odd, considering that research has failed to find a relation between sons with receding hairlines and mothers who sport sparse combovers. In any case, what does that have to do with those hideous tufts of coarse, sometimes barbed, hairs that seem to shoot out of every other orifice?

Blame it on testosterone. While some (and you know who you are) may postulate that follicles invert, or "turn in," after andropause, I lean toward the "dipstick theory" of selective hirsuteness. As discussed in chapter 2, testosterone is responsible for all body hair. As the hormone "burns off" and its level is reduced, it can no longer reach the top of his head. Still potent, testosterone runs amok in the regions available to it, stimulating and thickening the normally fine hairs in the ears and nose, and creating that noticeable "furring" on the upper back. While not directly threatening to his health (though watch out for yourself during lovemaking—some of those nose sprouts are as sharp as a Ginsu knife!), this phenomenon can greatly increase grooming time, particularly if these areas must be moussed to stay manageable.

But in an ironic twist of fate, testosterone also causes loss of head hair. An evil enzyme called 5-Alpha Reductase, which has headquarters on the scalp, converts the unsuspecting testosterone into another form, *dihydrotestosterone* (DHT), by showing up uninvited on its doorstep just after it has stepped out of the shower, then keeping it standing there dripping water on the welcome mat. As the enzyme forces copy after copy of the *Watchtower* into the testosterone's damp hands, the trusting and easily led hormone feels compelled to dress up in a suit and annoy others door to door.

No, wait. That's the Jehovah's Witnesses. But the process is very similar.

What happens next is that the powerful DHT degrades the innocent hair follicles, ordering them to clean the latrines with a toothbrush and making them run in unbearable heat carrying heavy combat gear while calling them "maggots" and "mamas' boys."

No. That's the United States Marines. But the process is very similar.

What actually happens is that the overbearing DHT causes the insecure hair follicles to regress to an almost infantile state—

you guessed it: just like your mother-in-law

—growing smaller and smaller until they produce only weak, fine, colorless hairs. Yes, that *is* the process.

So what is your man so upset about? He still has a full head of hair. It's just invisible.

4. MEMORY LOSS

For your man, this can be the most frustrating aspect of andropause. Often he will complain that he forgot his own address and then had to spend half the night at Rusty's Non-stop GoGo until his memory returned. As might be expected, his loved one exhibits skepticism, especially when he also cannot recall how those black silk panties came to be wrapped around his neck.

Since it has been shown that short-term memory can be improved through testosterone therapy, you can assume that some of these lapses are purely the result of insufficient hormone. But he'd be wise to come up with a better excuse before you clock him.

5. COLD FLASHES

He's sitting in a board meeting, trying to decide between giving up his yearly bonus or laying off 600 employees. Suddenly he feels a chill travel up his spine; perspiration begins to trickle down his collar. He hurriedly excuses himself. In the men's- room mirror his face looks pale, corpse-like. He splashes on some hot water to restore color, then tries to mop up what he's spilled on his pants so it won't look like he's had an "accident." When he returns to the meeting, he votes to pink-slip the entire East Coast division.

These episodic changes in temperature—the flip side to the menopausal female's hot flashes—may be triggered by hormones affecting the hypothalamus, or possibly the hypotenuse (I can't be sure; like many women, I wasn't encouraged to take science classes after the 11th grade). Though it has been noted that a cold flash is often accompanied by momentary panic in which the andropausal man feels his entire life is a sham, I will not entertain the idea that this is a cause-and-effect relationship. True, as he nears the peak of his personal and professional accomplishments, the middle-aged man often contemplates the meaningless of his existence, but these thoughts pass quickly, and he again remembers that HE CAN BEND ALL CREATURES TO HIS WILL. Swedish researchers would have us believe that cold flashes are the icy fingers of Death playing Tchaikovsky's "Pathetique" on his spine, but you know those Swedes can get pretty gloomy.

6. IRRITABILITY

About 60 percent of viropausal men exhibit marked crankiness. The remaining 40 percent live alone and so are never told how incredibly crabby they have become.

The source of this behavioral change...well, not "change" actually, but *intensification*...seems self-evident: he has difficulty sustaining arousal, he keeps forgetting to remove his wedding ring in bars, he can comb his nose hairs into a pompadour. Why shouldn't he be grumpy? But testosterone loss has something to do with it, too, providing more evidence of the origin of the word "testy."

At a 1995 meeting of the Endocrine Society,[36] researchers reported that men with a deficiency in testosterone described a feeling of edginess. Those given testosterone-replacement therapy reported a positive change of mood. Those who thought they were getting Grateful Dead tickets but were given testosterone-replacement therapy instead were really ticked off. Those who thought they were getting testosterone replacement but were actually given a Yoo-Hoo were happiest of all.

7. FATIGUE

At this time in your man's life he may tell you he's too exhausted to help with the dishes—and even *he* will be surprised to discover he's telling the truth. Reduced energy is reported by about 80 percent of viropausal men. Assume that the other 20 percent were napping and just didn't hear the question.

When this fatigue cannot be linked to obvious physical stresses—such as exercise, illness or operating heavy machinery when taking over-the-counter cold remedies—it

---

[36]A very exclusive society, by the way, with a very long waiting list and a secret handshake you don't want to know about. Motto: "This gland is your gland, this gland is my gland."

is thought to be brought about by biological changes in the aging brain. Some preliminary studies have tried to find a correlation between diminished energy and overdependence on TV remotes, but the research subjects were uncooperative and hostile during attempts to have the devices pried from their fingers.

8. DEPRESSION

Sex hormones are natural mood elevators, capable of transporting your man to the emotional equivalent of the top of the Empire State Building. As he ages and his testosterone loses power, however, he will often get stuck between floors or even wake up one morning to find the message: "Out of Order—Use the Stairs."

Only 70 percent of andropausal men will suffer from this disheartening condition; the other 30 percent will enjoy it. Bouts of despair, self-pity and gloom will be enlivened by periods of weeping, moaning and whining. As his loved one, you may find it difficult to be around him during these episodes, but this only leaves him free to socialize with others. However, after a while, even they will look surreptitiously at their wristwatches and tell him they are late for appointments elsewhere.

9. MUSCLE ATROPHY

Until now, your man's body has been supplying him with adequate hits of testosterone, Nature's First Steroid, and even computer geeks like Microsoft magnate Bill Gates may have been able to sustain some muscle tone up to this point. Unfortunately, the decrease in hormone leaves his biceps micro and soft, while other areas of his physique start to look like undigested cottage cheese, large curd.

Lifestyle changes at this stage are also a factor. In his younger days, as he loves to tell you, he naturally engaged in more physical labor—wrestling mountain lions, mining coal, lifting automobiles to save orphaned children pinned underneath. Now his most concentrated manual effort involves adjusting the incline settings on the LazyBoy.

Tell your man that he can counteract this deterioration of his manhood with regular resistance exercises—though up to now he has been regularly resisting exercise. It doesn't matter how old and puddinglike he is—it's never too late to start! Here's proof: In a Tufts University study, a group of nursing-home residents over age 90 were put on a weight-lifting program. (It sounds cruel, but the exercisers *were* supervised and tested daily to be sure they were using steroids.) After 12 weeks, not only did they increase their strength sevenfold, but one of the men was able to toss aside his walker and marry Maria Shriver.

10. INSOMNIA

Your man's body will have a decreased need for rest now. Having completed its life's work—building bone and tissue—it has nothing more strenuous to do than sit back and watch him die. Who could sleep?

4

The Toys of Autumn:
Accessorizing for Andropause

Sometimes a cigar is just a cigar.
—Sigmund Freud, before his cancer-ridden jaw had to be
surgically removed

In her very thick book The Change, feminist Germaine Greer noted, as she sat in a French bistro, that middle-aged women, as their allure fades, become almost ignored in our society. They are completely ignored when trying to catch the waiter's eye for a refill on their café au lait.

While andropausal men rarely write thick books on the subject, it's obvious that they, too, feel invisible—without any of the benefits of real invisibility, like being able to sneak into a football stadium without paying. So at this time, your man may start acquiring "objects." Subconsciously, he thinks they will increase his status or return him to his former glory. Consciously, he thinks they make him look really cool. Unfortunately, they only make him conspicuous, and not in a good way. Some of these accessories are merely bigger, louder, hairier, smellier versions of what he valued as a teenager. But now he is a teenager who has nearly $250,000 in his IRA.

Try to be sympathetic, keeping in mind that these external trappings are merely a cry to be noticed. As Linda, the wife of bespectacled, middle-aged Willie Loman, said in Arthur Miller's *Death of a Salesman,* "Attention must be paid!" And we all know how that story turned out: bespectacled, middle-aged Arthur Miller attracted Marilyn Monroe—and a lot of attention. So be grateful if your man's only interest is in one of the following nonblonde status symbols.

Auto Eroticism

A long, sleek, tumescent-red device that throbs with power and quickly pulls in and out of tight spots . . . What does your man see in a high-priced, high-performance car? Himself.

A little (the smaller, the better?) red sportscar[37] is practically the Red Badge of Courage to the viropausal man. Not long ago he wouldn't have walked into a dealership without first checking out a prospective car's *Consumer Reports* safety ratings, nor would he have driven out without a demonstration of its antilock brakes. Now the only standard feature he looks for is a roll bar. The irony is that he can finally afford the Lamborghini[38] he wished he had at 17, but getting in and out of it aggravates his high-school football injury.

Car advertising subliminally fuels the middle-aged man's fantasies. Some of the actors intoning the voiceovers have reached the age that, in some states, requires them to bring a doctor's note before they can get their driver's license renewed. Not so subliminally, the ads often show a leggy brunette, obviously not from the Department of Motor Vehicles, who seems to be trying to polish the car with her breasts.

But it's speed, not sex, that sells these cars. Your man is secretly hoping that once he has buckled himself into one of these land missiles, he can step on the accelerator, attain warp speed, smash through the sound barrier, travel through time and show up at his prom, the envy of the entire Class of '68.

---

[37]Or "menoPorsche," as one woman calls her ex-husband's new mode of transportation. I won' t repeat what she calls her ex-husband.
[38]Italian for "You'll be paying for this, one way or the other, for the rest of your life."

So don't be too hard on him. Even a man as successful and blue-eyed as Paul Newman took up auto racing[39] in his 40s. Perhaps you're just worried that your man may put himself in danger. But there's little chance of that. Like his aging body, these high-strung machines will spend most of the time in for repairs.

TEAM PLAYER

There was an unfortunate period in men's sartorial history during which every third male over 40 wore an Indiana Jones hat. If he were suddenly called away to find the Temple of Doom, he was dressed for it.

Now, judging by the number of men sporting baseball hats and team jackets, you'd think the Yankees were playing an away game every weekend and in every major city—and that the roster had been expanded to 10,000 players. Granted, some of the cap-wearing males are teenagers, but you can easily separate the men from the boys: those whose only hope is a spot in an Old-Timers game wear them brim- *forward.*

The caps are not limited to sport teams. Some men seem to be having their midlife anxiety sponsored by Valvoline; others who wouldn't know the difference between a thresher and a combine[40] are walking advertisements for John Deere. Whatever the logo, these hats deliver the same message: "I'm bald."

But even sports caps are more than the poor man's toupee. They are about belonging to some larger brotherhood, uniting young men and less-young men, rich and poor, in a mental hideaway where beer can be spilled, curses

---

[39]The technical term for driving around and around in circles very fast.
[40]You can thresh with a combine, but you can't combine with a thresher, and neither one makes an instant coffee that tastes good.

uttered and giant Styrofoam fingers waved. Here, the woes of middle age cannot find them—for at least four hours, or more if the game goes into overtime.

A few menopausal men—those with roughly 200 million extra dollars—may go a step farther and buy their own teams. They have attained the sports fan's ultimate dream: telling the players and coaches how to play ball. And certainly all those years of yelling at the TV set qualifies them for the major leagues.

HAIR APPARENT (MEN BEHAVING BALDLY)

Some thin-haired men, however, find that wearing a logo'd cap around the clock is impractical,[41] and most are looking for a more permanent solution. However, men lose all reason along with their hair. It's as if the smarter brain cells see their chance to escape through the open follicle: "Psst! I'm goin' over the skull tonight. Who's comin' with me? Just hold on to a root and we're outta here."

Perhaps because of the connection between hair growth and testosterone, men are convinced that hair somehow contains all of their Super Powers.[42] Without it, they will lose their magical ability to revive a stalled car by kicking the tires. (Though this automotive repair strategy hasn't worked yet, it does occupy him long enough for you to call AAA.)

So naturally, shampooing creates a tremendous conflict between men's already shaky interest in personal hygiene and their fear of dislodging a few more of their precious strands. When they see large clumps of their remaining hair in the bathtub drain, they feel a sense of loss so deep that they become immobilized. So they leave the hairs there,

---

[41]Say, when being sworn in as president of the United States, though not when jogging as one.

[42]At least those super powers not directly supervised by "Little Elvis."

hoping they will root, like leaf cuttings. (That's why they hate seeing *your* hair in the tub—they're afraid of cross-breeding.) And thus came the idea for hair transplants.

Unfortunately, the first attempts with foraged drain hair didn't take. So hair surgeons dug out live shrubs from the back of the head[43] and moved them to the desert regions, in some cases adding a gravel path, gazebo or other landscaping touches. So for a while, hair plugs were big. *Too* big— Cabbage Patch Dolls had smaller follicles. In addition, many of these transplants went horribly wrong and had to be prematurely harvested, leaving a scalp that looked like a geographical survey map of Mars but without the exciting discovery of past life forms. Recent infomercials reassure us that the process has improved. Still, watch out if your man drinks too much water; his perforated head may spurt like a lawn sprinkler.

Minoxidil (brand name: YOUR AD HERE) has been a godsend for many men. Applied twice a day, it miraculously delays, for at least a year, your man's realization that he has really, truly lost his hair and will never get it back.[44] Some men do wind up with a fuzzy growth that leaves the tops of their heads looking like lint traps. But minoxidil seems to work best on those who start out with just a small yarmulke-like bald spot. It would be quicker and less expensive if these men gracefully disguised their problem by converting to Judaism.

Actually, the substitute hair doesn't even have to look real. Desperation led some guy to invent spray-on hair—stucco for the scalp. Greater desperation has driven other guys to order it from an 800 number very late at night. Advertisers know these men are too tired and sedated with Cheetos to resist.

But when it comes to coverups, the CIA could learn a lot from balding men. The methods by which they try to extend

---

[43]Why not from the ears, which could use a little deforestation?

[44]Let's see: at about $30 per monthly treatment, times 12 months, times an estimated 3 million customers, that adds up to $1.08 billion that the executives of the pharmaceutical companies can use to get themselves the best toupees money can buy.

what little they have—rather like Hamburger Helper—are truly inventive and truly futile. Let's explore their methods further, so that we can classify them and create a common glossary. Then we can use these terms to ridicule other men, indirectly discouraging our own solar-paneled husbands from trying anything like these comb-overs. In chronological order:

THE ELVIS The front hairs are grown almost down to his chin, then swept back into a pompadour that loses momentum somewhere midhead. To enhance the illusion, he'll grow bushy sideburns and try to comb them into the exodus, too. Then he'll make himself a fried peanut-butter-and-banana sandwich and OD on the toilet. Not a pretty sight.

THE JULIUS CAESAR Hair is grown long at the back of the head, then coaxed forward over the bald spot into spiky, forehead-hugging bangs. He thinks this will fool Cleopatra. This only worked for Richard Burton.

THE TRAPDOOR Hairs are combed from one side across the bald spot, then shellacked with a "men's styling product." As each slight breeze blows, the mutually adhered hairs lift up as one unit, allowing just enough of an opening for illegal immigrants to sneak under before it slams shut once again.

THE BANJO Here, the remaining hairs are so few and far between and stretched across the skull so tightly that you can strum the theme song from *Deliverance*. Really, the only one who would find this hair arrangement eye-catching is Roy Clark, if he were still alive and picking. Oops! He is! So keep your man out of the Grand Ole Opry!

THE CAN'T PART So much of his hair has abandoned his head that nothing but a thin fringe runs above the collar, like algae washed up on the sands of time. But HE STILL HAS HAIR. He will grow one side long, run a part through it so far down that he risks puncturing his eardrum and drag these strands kicking and screaming over his dome. Only sheer will and a staple gun can possibly hold them in place, so inevitably a few long strands straggle down. People may be tempted to pull on them to see if his head lights up. Encourage them.

So you endure these tonsorial improvisations for a few years. Then it happens: He comes home one day, takes off his baseball cap, runs his fingers through his hair and can't get them out. You scream and call the Animal Control Bureau. Wrestling the phone from your shaking hands, he asks cheerfully, "What do you think of the toupee?"

Like organ transplants, this donor hair always appears in danger of being rejected. Even celebrities who could buy and sell Canada cannot find a realistic-looking hairpiece.[45] So how come they can put a man on the moon but they can't put a man on the moon in a toupee that looks natural even 238,857 miles from the Earth's surface? At least they could start with a cure for Toupee Tail—the cowlick that sticks up jauntily where the fake hair hits the shirt collar. (I never could watch *Evening Shade* without wanting to jump up and smooth the back of Burt Reynolds' head.)

Whichever hell toupee (a list of styles follows) your man brings home, don't let him keep it, even as a pet. He will become attached to it, even after it becomes too old to fetch his pipe and slippers.

THE DAVY CROCKET   Whether or not he "kill'd him a b'ar when he was only 3," your man shouldn't wear a pelt on his head. It looks like roadkill that crawled up on a bowling ball to die. But remember, it's only napping, so don't provoke it. Even more unnerving is if the toupee does not match the color of the original hair it is perched on—giving the unfortunate illusion of two badgers mating. In either case, if your

---

[45]The best rugs just spark conversations like: "Do you think he's wearing a toupee?" "No, I don't think so. Do you think he is?" "I don't know. Maybe." Rule of thumb: If you have to ask, it *is* one.

man has decided to supplement this hairpiece by growing the remainder of his hair into a ponytail, he's taken the coonskin cap thing too far. It's open season for ridicule. (Note to Casey Kasem: Once you've topped 40, this is not a Top 40 look.)

THE CHIA PET Spreading over the entire head, this woolly hairpiece looks as natural as a DisneyWorld topiary. Spray occasionally for aphids and do not overwater. (Note to several TV anchormen and reporters: just cover the news, not your head.)

THE MISTREATED POODLE Remember Burt Reynolds' sleek, dark—though sparse—hair in his Dan August days? Everybody does, so why would he think we'd fall for that curly headdress? Too bad Loni didn't get *all* the rugs in the divorce settlement.

THE TSUNAMI Sadly, this type—sweeping up forcefully from the forehead and curling forward in a dashing tidal wave effect—seems to have almost disappeared along with the late Jack Lord. But there may still be a few of these *Hawaii 5-0* models around. If you look closely, you may see little surfers hanging 10 on the hairline.

THE DIVOT It's easy to see how they came up with this. Two guys are playing golf. One guy takes a swing, knocks up a little thatch of lawn, which lands perfectly on the bald spot at the back his head. The other guy says, "Looks good." Par for the course. Actor Ted Danson had the self-respect to trash his Divot on TV—though only after the back of his head had appeared in the *National Enquirer* enough times to make it impossible to sue for slander.

THE EV'NING TIDE This gently receding rug looks like the last lap of ocean on a particularly smooth stretch of beach. It also seems to come and go on certain follicle-repressed movie stars, depending on whether the part calls for

Method hair. The "toupette" would be almost dignified, if it weren't so cowardly. Make a commitment, guys!

Interestingly, male-pattern baldness is also found in some primates—in particular, the stump-tailed macaques. After years of studying these Old World monkeys (natives of Southeast Asia and China), researchers from many disciplines have come to the same conclusion: No self-respecting macaque would be caught dead in a toupee. So much for evolution.

WAITING TO INHALE

"A woman is only a woman, but a good cigar is a smoke," wrote Rudyard Kipling [46] way before he inflicted *Gunga Din* on an unsuspecting public. His observation and the following (almost true) guidelines for selecting a cigar seem to give some insight into why this tobacco product is so popular among andropausal men.

1. Squeeze gently up and down; it should give but not be too soft.
2. Beware of lumps or soft spots. Inspect for discolorations, loosening or cracks; it should be smooth and tight, not damaged on either end or oozing pus.
3. Look for uneven wetness, which results when the unexposed side does not dry properly. To correct this, it should be "aged" for at least a week in a good-quality humidor or stewardess.
4. Check the exposed end. Some variation of color is normal, but not an extreme or abrupt

---

[46]Kipling was later arrested for soliciting a panatela.

color change—otherwise, you might experience an off-taste or a burning sensation during urination.

Perhaps this is why a man in his middle years often reaches for his well-aged Dominican Partagas.[47] As he caresses
the long, fat, smooth projectile, it's easy to assume a phallic
connection. But as he cuts off the end and sets fire to it, you
think, *Ow, that would hurt.*

So there must be more to a cigar than meets the eye and
nostrils. For those who favor contraband varieties from
Cuba, this daring indulgence may be the closest they get to
being a guerrilla fighter, even though the truth may be less
romantic—like the cigars were smuggled in through a sheep
stomach. If it's attention your man is after, the cigar will get
it for him. Women will sidle up to him in public places and
ask in a low, breathy whisper, "Would you please put that dis-
gusting thing out? It's triggering my asthma."[48]

More likely, the cigar acts as a cloaking device. The acrid
smoke encircles his head, sort of like the cloud cover over
Mount Kilimanjaro. Then everyone around him starts
squinting and coughing, further impairing their vision. So, as
with most of his efforts at this stage of his life, he has succeeded yet again in diverting us from his bald spot.

BIGGER, LONGER, WIDER

The subject of male menopause came up at a recent dinner
party. "I'll let you know when I get there," said the host,
whom I will call Mitch, since that is his name. Then he

---

[47]By the way, size *does* matter: the larger the diameter, the fuller the flavor; the longer the length, the cooler the smoke; and the deeper the
stench, the lonelier the smoker.

[48]This has led to the formation of cigar bars and "cigar nights" at restau-
rants, where like-minded aficionados gather to taste new brands, sip
cognac and exchange air fresheners.

ushered his guests into his rec room and slid a movie into his laser-disc player. On the drive-in-theater-sized TV screen, a long, fat, smooth nuclear submarine cut through a watery underworld. Thanks to Mitch's new Surround Sound stereo system, the blips from the movie sonar bounced off every wall and created a momentary panic at Groton Naval Base, 150 miles away. Finally, a voice broke through the eerie sound effects: "I don't understand this, sir—I'm picking up something strange. I'm gonna move her in a little closer to take a looooo . . . *ARGHHH! Glub, glub."*

There you have it: male menopause at its most technologically advanced. An abysmal film shown at the local multiplex for $6.75 can be watched at home for a mere $1,235.25, not counting popcorn and a beverage. After 183 viewings,[49] the system pays for itself. Mitch finally admitted, "The depth of the crisis is directly proportional to the wattage of the system."

This expansion of electronics is, of course, a throwback to the teenage stereo years. Only now, your man has entered adulthood, worked years of overtime and carefully invested his hard-earned savings into something even cooler than woofers and tweeters—subwoofers and titanium tweeters! A few more control panels, and he's re-created the Houston Space Center.

Eventually, your modest Cape Cod may resemble Radio Shack. He'll want to own the first remote-control snow-blower on your block—which will sit in the garage, since you live in Tucson. He will "help you out" by bringing home a garlic press with three speeds and a self-cleaning feature; through the wonders of space-age technology, it will get the same job done in twice the time at seven times the cost and take up half your counter space. Many of these gadgets will be just that—more complex versions of what he already has,

---

[49] Of the same movie, since few films are currently available on laser disc. Even if there were more, only 36 films worth viewing have been produced since *The Birth of a Nation* premiered in 1915. The movie Mitch has is not one of them.

with bigger knobs. He thinks he needs them to upgrade his system. You know he needs them to aid his failing eyesight.

THE FAMILY JEWELS

In some primitive cultures, a young woman who reaches marriageable age must walk through her native village balancing all her worldly possessions on her head. This ritual establishes her worth and, hopefully, attracts an equally well-endowed suitor. Sometimes the ritual ends tragically when, loaded down with her household goods, the young woman is trampled by stampeding elephants.

If your man already has a precariously balanced toupee, he may need to find another way to show his net worth. If he brings home a small velvet box, you can bet it won't be for you. He may wrap his neck in enough gold chains to anchor *Queen Elizabeth II* (both the ship and the monarch), or his taste may run to platinum cuff links, a ruby-studded pinky ring or a diamond tiara. More likely he will decide to trade up his wristwatch, even though—and I may be wrong about this as I don't own one—a $2,000 Rolex isn't any more effective than a $29.95 Timex at slowing down aging.

While this glittery show may seem a little tacky, don't discourage these purchases. Jewelry doesn't depreciate as much as a hairpiece, Cuban Hoyo, Corvette or Dolby home theater. It can more readily be accounted as community property. And, most importantly, it is not as easily crushed by stampeding elephants.

5

Smart Men, Foolish Hormones

Men have become tools of their tools.
—Henry David Thoreau

*A*t the age of 54, my birth mother[50] dropped off her car for a tune-up at a Sears Automotive Center in a mall near her home. After an hour or so of shopping, she returned, only to be told that the car wasn't ready. She went back into the mall and treated herself to lunch at JC Penney.[51] At Sears an hour later, the car was still up on the lift. Frustrated and feeling a loss of control perhaps, she again wandered the mall. That's when she noticed the sign: FREE EARRINGS WITH $10 EAR PIERCING.

Until then Mom had managed to make it through most of her adult life and a variety of formal social occasions wearing clip-ons, refusing to take part in what she thought of as self-mutilation. But that day, she gave in to her secret primitive urge and returned home with her lobes bored and fitted with surgical-steel posts. After the shock and the talk of involuntary commitment had subsided, the family calmed down and accepted her transformation. Later we came to welcome it, since it expanded our options for birthday and Christmas gifts—and frankly, we had begun to run out of ideas.

The point of this story? To publicly embarrass my mother.

---

[50]Actually, she's my only mother, but in these times, it seems mandatory to make the distinction.
[51]The names of the stores have been changed to protect her credit rating.

But also to demonstrate that when women in midlife give in to hormonal urges, they rarely topple governments, break up families or need to be served with subpoenas. But what if my mom had been the Leader of the Free World? What if, say, Richard Nixon had had a few hours—or even 18 minutes—to kill in 1971 and had emerged from a mall wearing a pair of gold hoops or diamond solitaires? I think we can conclude with assurance that:

> **1.** He would not have been elected to a second term.
> **2.** The military's "don't ask, don't tell" policy would have been mandated two decades earlier.
> **3.** The country would have been spared seeing "-gate" added to every pseudoscandal for the next 25 years.

Andropause may have turned your usually sensible male into an insensate mule, but consider Hannibal and Napoleon. They might have settled down and become doting grandfathers instead of political exiles if not for their last-ditch attempts to recapture their youth (along with a new empire). Catastrophic coups, financial fiascoes, political posturing and long-winded literature are all in a day's work for men unable to accept their diminishing power. From Adam ("She gave me of the tree and I did eat") to Allen ("She gave me the Polaroid and I did shoot"), from Dante ("In the middle of the road of life/I found myself in a dark wood") to Dole ("I'm middle of the road. Really."), aging men have made history, for better or worse. Here are just 25 in the Andropausal Man's Hall of Shame:

ADAM (Genesis 1:26–5:3) It all began when God said: "Be fruitful, multiply, fill the earth and conquer it" (Jerusalem Bible version) and Adam took him literally. He got to name everything, so he started with his penis, which he called

Richard. Then God said He was going out for ribs, and the next thing Adam knew, in the biblical sense, was Eve. All in all, Adam had everything a man could want. What else but a midlife crisis would have driven Adam to take a bite of the forbidden fruit? He wasn't tricked into it; he was standing right next to Eve when she plucked the fruit from the Tree of the Knowledge of Good and Evil.[52] Okay, maybe his thoughts were elsewhere—probably reconsidering his decision earlier that day to call the long-nosed, ant-eating beast an *aardvark.* "Perhaps *Ralph* would be a better name," he was thinking when Eve said, "Here, can I tempt you?" Maybe he thought Eve had said, "Does this taste fresh to you?" as she often did. But when God confronted them, Adam naturally took no responsibility. "The woman whom thou gavest to be with me, she gave me of the tree and I did eat," he said, blaming Eve and God in one shot. Naturally, God drove them out of the Garden and into the suburbs.[53] After this incident, Adam would have gone off to have an affair, but there were no other women around. So he had to content himself with calling Eve a pain in his side for the rest of his life, which turned out to be 930 years.

SAMSON (Judges 13–16) He had superhuman strength, great hair and a comfortable judgeship but lost it all trying to impress a little Philistine named Delilah. First he lost his hair, then his eyesight. Then his hair grew back only to give him enough strength to bring the house down on everyone, including himself. Middle-aged men should have learned more from this myth than "Hair Is Power."

---

[52]Adam had wanted to call the tree something simpler, like *Mr. Farnsworth,* but God had the last word on that one.

[53]Eating the fruit of the Tree of Knowledge, etc., obviously didn't boost their IQs that much since the only thing they realized was that they weren't properly dressed. So they sewed some fig leaves together for loincloths, but Eve criticized Adam's stitches and Man has never so much as replaced a button since.

KING DAVID (reigned 1012–972 B.C.) He slew Goliath with a single pebble to the temple, but when the little shepherd boy who became king of Israel eventually became old and stricken, he was the one with rocks in his head. He lost the spring in his sling—or, as the Bible puts it, "gat no heat." So his servants gave him a lovely young virgin named Abishag, and the inscription on the gift card read, "Let her cherish him and let her lie in thy bosom, that my lord the king may get heat." Despite her cherishing and lying, the king still "knew her not," content to spend their nights together playing Scrabble.[54] Meanwhile, one of his sons, Adonijah, took advantage of David's infirmity by going around telling everyone *he* was king. And still David didn't catch on—or, as the Bible says, "knowest it not." So another of his sons, Solomon, who would become revered for his wisdom, had his elderly father declared "incompetent" and "becameth" king himself.

HANNIBAL (247–182? B.C.) As usual, male historians have exaggerated the strategic skills of this general, who actually went AWOL from the Carthaginian Army to join the circus. Though he made a wrong turn over the Alps with his performing elephants and accidentally invaded Italy, he was able to turn this into a series of military triumphs. At 45, he suffered his first major defeat in North Africa, somehow losing 20,000 men without injury to himself (perhaps the military term "deserter" might be appropriate here, hmm?). He tried a few comebacks but succeeded only in irritating the Romans, who demanded he surrender. Instead Hannibal poisoned himself, possibly by eating oysters out of season.

JULIUS CAESAR (100–44 B.C.) In 48 B.C., the 52-year-old Roman statesman had his dalliance with the 21-year-old Cleopatra,

---

[54]Whenever she landed on a Triple Word Score, he would taunt her by rhyming Abishag with "a dish rag" or even "a big hag." But she didn't care because she had access to his credit cards.

later setting her up in a little Roman love nest. (Caesar's account of a later military victory—"I came, I saw, I conquered"—is thought to repeat a review of his first night with Cleo, though in a slightly different order of action.) Then when he was 54 years old, he reformed the Roman calendar so he would be only 39. His judgment impaired by his sex-addled brain, he gave amnesty to his former enemies; since the FTD "Thanks a Bunch" bouquet hadn't been invented yet, they were forced to show their appreciation by assassinating him on the Ides of March.[55] Tragically, Caesar never got a chance to tell his protégé Marc Antony to steer clear of Cleo, so she was able to repeat her pyramid scheme. Too impatient to wait for an assassination, Antony committed suicide by drinking Caesar salad dressing made with an undercoddled egg.

GENGHIS KHAN (A.D. 1167?–1227) Having achieved his goal of being named Genghis Khan (meaning "CEO" in the local dialect) of the Mongolian Empire at age 39, the warrior Temujin went about aimlessly conquering the rest of the continent. He was so barbarous, he used civilians as living shields, massacred whole villages without provocation, drank red wine with fish and gave everyone bad haircuts. Afraid of dying, Genghis consulted a Taoist priest to learn how to become immortal, which seemed to involve having his portrait painted on black velvet. On his last campaign to invade China, Mr. Tough Guy fell off his horse while hunting and died asking for a side order of Szechuan pork.

DANTE ALIGHIERI (1265–1321) After failing in his political ambitions, the middle-aged Middle Ages poet began his famous work, *The Divine Comedy,* at 42. The first of the poem's three parts, *The Inferno,* shows us that midlife is, literally and literarily, hell; it starts by describing the half-dead

---

[55]His last words, "Et tu, Bruté?" mean, of course, "What's an Ides?"

poet wandering lost in a dark wood, his way blocked by the Leopard of Malice and Fraud, the Lion of Violence and Ambition, the She-Wolf of Incontinence and the Wildebeest of Sciatica. He then encounters the completely dead poet Virgil who forces him to listen to his off-color limericks, then guides him through a deep chasm divided into nine circles. Here, Dante is introduced to famous people, each one's behavior more despicable than the next, the farther down he goes. On the lowest circle, farthest away from God, Dante meets Geraldo Rivera. Later, Dante dies of malaria, probably contracted by practicing his backstroke in the notoriously polluted canals of Venice.

CHRISTOPHER COLUMBUS (1451–1506) History has proven that the wanderlust experienced by andropausal men can result in some prime real estate. Columbus was 42 when he set sail from Spain in 1492 and, like some Australian film stars of today, landed in America entirely by accident. The idea of getting to the East by going west should have warned off everyone, as should his boast: "Neither reason nor mathematics nor maps were any use to me." Not surprising, then, that he was never sure where he was: when he sighted Cuba, he made his crew swear, on penalty of having their tongues pulled out and made into deli sandwiches, that Cuba was the mainland; then he saw the mainland and called it an island. Go figure. He later returned to Spain in chains after a little mishap in Haiti (his diary insists it was over a cocktail waitress). Attempts to regain his prestige took him as far as Honduras before he ran out of traveler's checks. He started hearing voices, none of which spoke his native language, and died, not on Columbus Day as he'd wished, but, ironically, on Amerigo Vespucci Day.[56]

---

[56]Vespucci, by the way, was a business manager until age 43, when he suddenly decided—oh, that demon andropause—to become a navigator. The continent of Vespucci is named after him.

NICCOLÒ MACHIAVELLI (1469–1527) At age 43, this Italian statesman lost his civil-service job, was run out of town, imprisoned, then released to poverty. Understandably disgruntled, he wrote his most famous book, *The Prince*.[57] (Its analysis of the unscrupulous assumption of political power gave us the term *Machiavellian,* which has only recently been replaced by *Gingrichian.*) This put him back in favor for a time. However, his publisher was less than scrupulous in remitting his royalties, and he died in Neglect, a small village north of Florence.

HENRY VIII (1491–1547) Handsome, trim and athletic as a young man, this King of England eventually became so obese he was called Henry the Ate Everything He Could Get His Hands On. At age 42, he had his marriage to Catherine of Aragon annulled so he could marry the gorgeous Anne Boleyn, 16 years his junior. When Anne, too, failed to produce a son for him, he had her beheaded, it having slipped his mind that he had the power to divorce her. He then married Jane Seymour, 27, whom he affectionately called "Dr. Quinn, Medicine Woman"; she not only gave him the son he hoped for, but she conveniently died in childbirth, saving the taxpayers the cost of another beheading. Married Anne of Cleves, 25; remembered to divorce her. Married Catherine Howard, 25; not wanting to look flighty, had her head handed to her. His last wife, 31-year-old Catherine Parr, had the foresight to stay out of Henry's way for three years until he died, as was only fitting, of syphilis and cirrhosis of the liver.

NAPOLEON (1769–1821) His hair receding at an early age didn't improve his disposition, especially when he found out others were calling him *petit tondu,* "little crop head," behind his back. But it only made him more determined to become emperor king, which he did at age 35. At 41 he divorced

---

[57]The title has since been changed to an unpronounceable symbol and is often referred to as "The Book Formerly Known as *The Prince.*"

46-year-old Josephine and married a 19-year-old archduchess. At 45, he was exiled to the isle of Elba—famous for its toast until the isle of Melba stole the recipe. When Napoleon realized his new wife was seeing someone else and his pension was about to be cut off, he tried and failed to rebuild his empire. This resulted in the Hundred Days campaign, which everyone said felt more like Three Hundred. Exiled to yet another island, he spent his remaining days sleeping late, playing cards and composing palindromes such as ABLE WAS I ERE I SAW ELBA. However, cream-filled pastries proved to be his Waterloo, and he died of stomach trouble.

PAUL GAUGUIN (1848–1903) After quitting his job as a stockbroker in Paris, the artist ran away to Tahiti at age 43, leaving behind his wife and children, several thousand francs in bistro tabs and a bad impression. So he decided to become a good Impressionist, and when that didn't work out, became a Postimpressionist. That seemed to suit him better, as it involved painting lots of bare-breasted Tahitian women. He died a miserable, painful death, but with a smile on his face.

ADOLF HITLER (1889–1945) It's incredible to think of the horrors that could have been averted if Hitler had been accepted to his first-choice school, The Academy of Fine Arts in Vienna. Instead of *Mein Kampf*,[58] he could have written self-important biographical notes for the program to his art-gallery showing. So, as with most men who have no other talents, he went into politics. At 42 he took 19-year-old shop assistant Eva Braun as his mistress. At 44 he became leader of the Third Reich *without* having had a personal-image consultant to talk him out of the silly mustache and comb-over. Then what's the first thing he does? Invades Austria to get back at the art-school administrators who had rejected him and called him *Schicklgruber.*[59] Hitler was also an early

---

[58]Translation: *I'm Nuts.*
[59]From the colloquial Austrian: *He's really nuts.*

pioneer of hormone replacement therapy, ordering German scientists to find a way to give testosterone booster shots to his army. Thankfully, they failed in their attempts, but, unfortunately, that didn't stop them from starting a fuhrer.

ERNEST HEMINGWAY (1899–1961) Though he dipped his quill in the font of testosterone and went through women like ink blotters, the big-game hunting, bullfight-loving writer didn't take well to physical decline. You don't need Cliffs Notes to guess what Hemingway was feeling at 53 when he wrote *The Old Man and the Sea,* the story of an aging fisherman who endures a long struggle to land a monstrous marlin, only to have it devoured by sharks on the way home.[60] Though this book won the Pulitzer Prize, Hemingway spent the remainder of his life denying that the marlin in the story represented his penis, which he called *Marlon.* After his third wife left him, he found a younger wife and lost himself in alcoholism. That may account for his mistaking his own tonsils for a charging rhino.

PABLO PICASSO (1881–1973) Despite his many mistresses, in later life Picasso suffered from impotence as the result of an untreated prostate condition. Ashamed to face women, he forgot what they looked like and mistakenly painted eyes on their chins and noses on their foreheads. If only he had used his artistic genius for good instead of evil.

ELVIS (1935–   ) The real tragedy is not so much that "The King" entered middle age with a paunch, Liberace-like jumpsuits and exaggerated "young Elvis" hair, but that he so unconvincingly faked his own death. He should have known that eventually he would be sighted at convenience stores, ATMs and gas stations. It's okay, Elvis. All is forgiven. You can come out now.

---

[60]Source: Cliffs Notes.

JOHN Z. DELOREAN (1925–) Remember him? When he reached middle age, this former General Motors hotshot didn't just buy a sportscar, he created his own company to *build* the *perfect* sportscar with his name on it. After six years in the planning, the first DeLorean (the wheels) rolled off the conveyor belt in 1981, about the time DeLorean (the wheeler-dealer) rolled into court to face charges of conspiring to distribute cocaine. (Hey, it wasn't easy getting financing for high-risk schemes in the 1980s.) He was acquitted of that charge as well as of embezzling $8.5 million from investors. In the process, though, he lost his car factory and his supermodel wife, Cristina Ferrare. About 6,000 DeLoreans are still on the go, but the original is not—tragically, he retired to New Jersey.

THE REVEREND JIM BAKKER (1940–) You could almost forgive this teleminister his hanky-panky with church secretary Jessica Hahn once you saw his wife, The Avon Lady from Hell. But it's not nice to defraud the Lord by diverting funds meant for good works, and a really great roller coaster at Heritage U.S.A., into an air-conditioned residence for his dog. Even if he could claim he was dyslexic and had read "dog" backward, he was looking for trouble from a Higher Authority than the IRS.

GARY HART (1937–) A Colorado senator should have known that you can't say "nyah-nyah, nyah-nyah, nyah" to the Washington press corps and get away with it. So when the promising Democratic presidential candidate of 1988 dared reporters to catch him in monkey business, they caught him on *Monkey Business,* the yacht that might as well have washed him up on Gilligan's Island. His 26-year-old cruise director, Donna Rice, went on to model No Excuses jeans, while Hart had plenty of excuses for what happened to his standing in the polls. In the year before the election, he withdrew, then re-entered, then withdrew—not an effective form of birth control but a great way to abort a political career.

MICHAEL MILKEN (1947–) Chalk up the greedy misdeeds of the 1980s to this generation's coming-of-middle-age men. All those insider tradings, pyramid schemes and S&L collapses can be traced to the first crop of boomer boys who risked it all—often other people's all—in wild attempts to make the last Big Score. Never mind that they already made $550 million a year—they just felt so *empty* inside. Milken suffered the most: he wasn't allowed to wear his toupee in prison. He now hopes to make restitution—but not a profit?— from his educational foundation. At least it'll keep him off the Street.

PRINCE CHARLES (1948–) Only the British could produce a middle-aged man so confused that he preferred a kipper-faced 40-something to his glamorous 13-years-younger bride. And they say King George was mad! Charles' behavior ought to discourage the Royal Family's practice of inbreeding once and for all.

SOL WACHTLER (1930–) When this 62-year-old man started his barrage of threatening letters and phone calls to his 17-years-younger mistress in 1992, he had to know his actions were illegal. After all, he *was* the chief judge of New York State's Court of Appeals. Unluckily for him, the FBI set him straight on some points of law. Commenting in *Newsweek* on how successful men respond to failure (professional or sexual), one psychiatrist said: "When their sense of power is pierced, these individuals often try to recapture it through very inappropriate means." The cowboy hat Wachtler wore to deliver his blackmail notes was definitely inappropriate; he should have worn a deerstalker. Actually, this downfall of a formerly well-respected jurist is so sad, I can't keep making fun of the guy. So let's move on to:

WOODY ALLEN (1935–) Oddly, this formerly distinguished filmmaker seems never to have heard the expression "a picture is worth a thousand words." As the 1992 Polaroids of his girlfriend's 19-year-old adopted daughter proved, one of those words was "pervert." Mia Farrow later accused him of needing more and more help to get a woody, but he really needed more and more help from his ever-present therapist. No matter how he has tried to justify his actions, who can ever again see one of his movies—usually featuring himself as the sweaty-fingered, sexually inadequate, arrested-adolescent love interest of a younger, much more attractive woman—without thinking, "So what is this? A documentary?"

BOB PACKWOOD (1937–) No record of middle-aged silliness would be complete without the diaries of this senator from Oregon, which were leaked in 1995. His self-deluded jottings about stealing kisses, trying different hairstyles and tuning out during boring lectures sounded oddly familiar. If Packwood hadn't mentioned Phil Gramm, you'd swear the journals were written by Gidget. Unfortunately, mentioning Phil Gramm led to a stronger punishment than just being grounded—he was kicked out of the House. No more voting on bills for you, young man, until you learn some responsibility.

BOB DOLE (1926 B.C.–) He may not have become president, but he is winner of the Longest–Running Midlife Crisis in History Medal of Honor. For two decades he was so desperate to get into the White House that he began referring to himself in the third person so he could nominate himself. In his last attempt on the presidency, this real-life grumpy old man would have done anything, even claim that he was a moderate. Yet would it have killed him to, just once, smile with *both* sides of his face? Now that he has heeded the call of 285 million Americans and dropped out of politics, he's doing so many comic turns on TV shows and commercials it's like he's auditioning for vaudeville. Too late again, Bob.

6

His Willy, His Self

*Most of our information comes from experiments on
animals other than human beings, but even with our
fragmentary information about man, there is no doubt that
the development and maintenance of normal sexual drive
and behavior is testosterone dependent and may be seriously
impaired by castration.*
—From *Human Physiology: The Mechanisms of Body Function*

———

*T*he textbook above was published in 1970, but more
recent research conducted by Dr. Lorena Bobbitt indicates
that removal of the male sex organ can cause more serious
impairment than was previously thought. Though her experiment was too limited to draw universal conclusions, early
results show castration may turn your man, like Dr. Bobbitt's
test subject, into a Las Vegas wedding-chapel minister.

But what if your man only *feels* like he's been castrated?
He's losing power everywhere else: at work, as younger men
surpass him in job performance; at home, as your son has his
eyelids pierced despite his father's order against it; and at his
doctor's, as he is forced to submit to a body-cavity search
more thorough than anything performed by an agent of the
Federal Drug Enforcement Agency.

Yet as degrading as these humiliations are, nothing makes
a man feel more impotent than impotence. Because he iden-
tifies so closely with his penis (see chapter 2, and any novel
by Norman Mailer), when *it* fails, *he* fails. As mentioned, this

can lead to the psychic numbness that forces him to seek stimulation through financial, physical or sexual risk-taking that he hopes will make him feel excited, alive, daring, powerful, aroused, attractive . . . *something.* Then the police or paramedics arrive and subject him to another cavity search.

The first time your *Homo* fails to become *erectus,* he will react as if he has lost a loved one. Most probably he will enter what psychologists call The 5 Stages of Grief:

> *Stage 1.* Denial: "I can't believe this is happening."
> *Stage 2.* Anger: "Shit! I can't *believe* this is happening!!"
> *Stage 3.* Acceptance: "I accept that if my wife hadn't let herself go, this *wouldn't* be happening."
> *Stage 4.* Adjustment: "I've adjusted by dumping my wife for a 16-year-old Olympic gymnast who can wrap her legs around her own head, so *why is this still happening!?*"
> *Stage 5.* Alcoholism: "I need a stiff drink."

When the National Institutes of Health Consensus Development Conference convened in 1992, the subject of impotence so disturbed this panel of health experts that its first decision was to change the term "impotence" to "erectile dysfunction." Then the panel went out to a nudie bar for lunch.[61] Okay, maybe it didn't, but it certainly needed a stiff drink after estimating that 10 to 20 million American men experience impot...*erectile dysfunction.* Make that 30 million, if you can count those that suffer from occasional impo...*erectile dysfunction.* And the panel probably stayed for the floor show once it

---

[61]Except for the one female member of the panel, who probably stayed behind to call all her girlfriends and laugh at how the men reacted when she suggested the term "Dead-eye Dick" or "Mr. Softy" instead.

realized that only 5 million of these imp...*erectile dysfunctional* men ever seek professional help—or at least the kind of professional help not named Lola.

Getting softer seems to correlate with getting older: of the 1,290 subjects taking part in the ongoing Massachusetts Male Aging Study, 22 percent of the 40-year-olds experienced at least occasional im...*erectile dysfunction*. The percentage kept rising (or rather, didn't rise) until it swelled (or rather, didn't swell) to 49 percent of 70-year-olds.

Now, your man may not admit that he is a Massachusetts Male. "I'm from Wisconsin!" he may say. "And we Wisconsineers don't know the meaning of the phrase 'erectile dysfunction'!" But you're with him in the bedroom when his engine stalls, and though he may make some excuse like "It wasn't properly serviced" or "The sun was in my eyes," you know better. This is the shape of things to come.

The problem often is *not* just that he's running low on testosterone, the dealer-authorized mechanic for his sex drive. His parts, now long past their warranty, are wearing out. Yes, aging—as demonstrated in the diagram on the next page and in experiments using various types of cheeses—stinks.

Medical researchers are finding that i...*erectile dysfunction* doesn't occur just because your man is getting older. It's because his *body* is getting older. And because he has been so fixated on the top of his head, he hasn't noticed. In fact, experts estimate that 85 percent of cases of *erectile dys*—oh, let's just call it what it is, IMPOTENCE!—are caused by other health problems. The remaining 15 percent are caused by phone calls from his mother.

Unrestricted blood flow to the penis is essential for achieving and maintaining an erection. Yet by middle age, a lifetime of poor eating habits has caught up with him—his entire circulatory system now resembles the checkout counter of a 7-Eleven. What chance do his corpuscles have of getting through to his "senior partner" when they come up against a dam of Pringles and Slim Jims stuck together with Cheez-Whiz?

I Am Joe's Rapidly Decaying Body

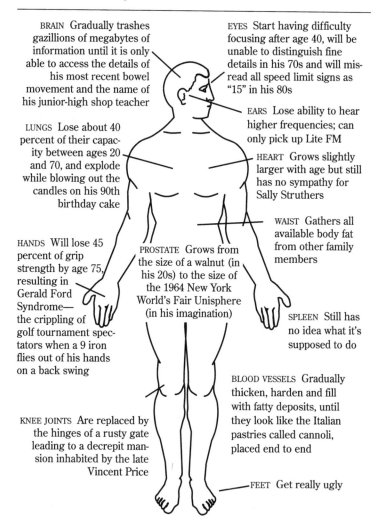

BRAIN Gradually trashes gazillions of megabytes of information until it is only able to access the details of his most recent bowel movement and the name of his junior-high shop teacher

LUNGS Lose about 40 percent of their capacity between ages 20 and 70, and explode while blowing out the candles on his 90th birthday cake

HANDS Will lose 45 percent of grip strength by age 75, resulting in Gerald Ford Syndrome—the crippling of golf tournament spectators when a 9 iron flies out of his hands on a back swing

KNEE JOINTS Are replaced by the hinges of a rusty gate leading to a decrepit mansion inhabited by the late Vincent Price

EYES Start having difficulty focusing after age 40, will be unable to distinguish fine details in his 70s and will misread all speed limit signs as "15" in his 80s

EARS Lose ability to hear higher frequencies; can only pick up Lite FM

HEART Grows slightly larger with age but still has no sympathy for Sally Struthers

WAIST Gathers all available body fat from other family members

PROSTATE Grows from the size of a walnut (in his 20s) to the size of the 1964 New York World's Fair Unisphere (in his imagination)

SPLEEN Still has no idea what it's supposed to do

BLOOD VESSELS Gradually thicken, harden and fill with fatty deposits, until they look like the Italian pastries called cannoli, placed end to end

FEET Get really ugly

SKIN Discolors from a lifetime of exposure to the sun, developing so many liver spots[62] that when he wears Bermuda shorts, with black socks and sandals, stray cats follow him and lick his calves

---

[62]Hint *not* from Heloise: To cover up liver spots, wrap in bacon.

As he gets older, your man may develop diabetes, which can lead to nerve damage. This can prevent the signals for arousal from reaching his "master switch." If his doctor then puts him on a sugar-restricted diet, he may become more obsessed with Ring Dings than with his "dingaling."

Generally, an unhealthy lifestyle, including smoking and the use of recreational drugs without partaking in any actual recreation, interferes with blood flow and contributes to a "leadless pencil." If your man is already on legal medications such as blood pressure pills or Jack Daniels, these can depress his nervous system—and along with it, his "pneumatic drill." This side effect will disturb him so much that, even if the prescribed medication is the only thing that keeps his heart beating, he will stop taking it right away because he believes death is preferable to impotence.[63]

Which leads us to his prostate. Though your man doesn't know where it is[64] and doesn't want to know, he will spend much of the rest of his life worrying about this tiny gland.[65] And if it becomes so enlarged that it puts his bladder in a headlock, he doesn't even want to hear about the procedure used to correct it, which doctors affectionately call "Roto-Rooter."[66] And God forbid if he has a more serious prostate illness. In a 1997 *Archives of Family Medicine* survey, 7 out of 10 men said they would prefer not to undergo annual prostate cancer screening and would let the cancer go untreated rather than risk impotence or other side effects of radiation or surgery. The other three men hurriedly excused themselves from the room as soon as they heard the word *prostate.*

---

[63]From *Women Wear Bras, Men Have a Penis: Further Explorations of the Differences Between the Sexes,* by Dr. M.J. Farawell.

[64]Sadly, men were never instructed to use a mirror, a flashlight and a plastic speculum to become familiar with their private parts, as we women were encouraged to do in *Our Bodies, Our Selves.*

[65]The first symptom of a problem: pronouncing prostate *prostrate.*

[66]Too bad, because it has an interesting aftereffect: during ejaculation, semen shoots in the opposite direction—into his own bladder. Why this surgery isn't performed more often as a form of birth control just shows how male-dominated the medical profession is.

Fixing Mr. Fix-It

If you can actually get your man to see a doctor, he will find that there are many solutions to impotence. He can take charge of his overall health himself—which he is sure to do only on the day earthworms wear tuxedos—or he can take advantage of these sophisticated and horrifying medical treatments:

INJECTION THERAPY Can you picture him, just before bringing you to the heights of ecstasy, plunging a hypodermic needle into his "tube steak"? Actually, can you picture him bringing you to the heights of ecstasy? If so, hold that image. It may be all you have for a while. But your man may decide this isn't such a bad treatment when you tell him it has a rare but reassuring side effect. The injected drug, which opens up blood vessels in his penis, can cause priapism—a constant erection. Unfortunately, it can also cause irreversible tissue damage, but except for having to wear pleated pants forever, what man wouldn't think it was worth the risk? It will make him feel 13 again.

PENILE IMPLANTS Two prostheses are surgically inserted on either side of the penis, like a permanent splint. They come in four models: malleable, semirigid, inflatable and dirigible. Make him spring for the malleable type: it's a silicone rod that can be bent like a Gumby until you find the right angle that hits your G spot. He might feel more natural with the inflatable type—a tiny pump is used to plump up the cylinder when needed. However, be sure he doesn't overinflate or he could wind up floating down New York's Fifth Avenue during the Macy's Thanksgiving Day parade. Should the inflation device malfunction, the air hose at the local Texaco can be used in a pinch.

VACUUM ERECTION DEVICE Now, this one sounds like hours of fun for both of you, since the hardware requires two people with the coordination of the West Point drill team. He slips into a plastic cylinder attached to a battery- or man-powered pump; this creates a vacuum that pulls blood, but hopefully not his kidneys, into his penis. Once a mutually acceptable grade of stiffness has been achieved, one of you slips a rubber band over the base of his penis to keep his "little soldier" at attention. *Don't* try this at home with your Electrolux and a scrunchie.

PENIS TRANSPLANT I heard this was featured on a *Jenny Jones* segment, which I didn't see. But I suspect if this catches on there will be a rash of kidnappings of involuntary organ donors, particularly Wilt Chamberlain.

ORAL DRUGS Though yohimbine, a traditional African aphrodisiac, has been approved by the FDA, it hasn't been very successful in treating impotence and may cause your man to insist that everyone call him Mandingo. Health-food stores also push ginseng and *avena sativa* (literally, wild oats), knowing men would buy anything labeled MAXIMUM-STRENGTH, SUPER-HIGH-POTENCY, SO-POWERFUL-YOUR-SPERM-WILL-BLAST-HOLES-THROUGH-GRANITE FORMULA. And mail-order ads in the back of men's magazines promote the powers of ground elk antlers and grizzly-bear pancreases—which must work because you almost never see elk and grizzlies at sex-therapy clinics.

SEX-THERAPY CLINICS Often the cause is simply all in your man's head—the *other* one. As all his physical processes start to slow down, it's only natural that he might need more time and a team of Swedish masseuses to become aroused. But if your man experiences a problem once, he may become insecure and doubt his potency. This leads to performance anxiety, so he'll be less likely to have a successful liftoff next time, and eventually may decide to scrub the entire mission, while the ground crew (you) waits below. Talking out his fears with you and an experienced, board-certified sex therapist would be as welcome to him as discussing his childhood bed-wetting in his alumni newsletter, so if you just make the appointment, you might solve the problem instantly. (HIM: "Look—see? It was just resting. Now can we get on with it? But first, call and cancel with Dr. Schlongmender.")

If these methods or the self-help techniques in the next chapter don't work, you may try to reassure him with the following observation from Paul T. Costa Jr., a psychologist at the National Institute on Aging in Washington, D.C.: "Some older men may say their erections aren't as big as they recall them being," Dr Costa Jr. told a *New York Times* reporter. "But then their partners say, 'Well, dear, you overestimated them back then, too.'"

An amusing point, and probably one many women can relate to, but inappropriate—the *New York Times* reporter had only been asking Dr. Costa if he could direct her to the Washington Monument.

7

I'm Okay—You, On the Other Hand, Need Lots of Help: What You Can Do for Him/What He Can Do to Himself

Will it give men shorter but possibly happier lives?
—hormone expert Dr. Richard Spark, on the practice of treating middle-aged men with testosterone even though it raises the risk of prostate cancer[67]

*A*lmost as soon as they get their first hot flash, menopausal women are advised to start hormone replacement therapy. Premarin, a "natural" estrogen drug, has become the most prescribed medication in America, despite the reported risk of breast cancer and the fact that it gets its name from its source: PREgnant MAre uRINe. But many middle-aged women claim that Premarin works wonders in relieving their symptoms, and they feel so much better that they can't wait to be saddled up for the Kentucky Derby.

Wouldn't it be wonderful if your man's andropausal symptoms could be cured by a possibly life-threatening drug, too? Well, rest assured that pharmaceutical companies have been working feverishly to exploit the insecurities and tap into the bank accounts of male baby boomers as well. While none bears

---

[67]He might as well have asked: "Why would parents with the last name Spark give their son a first name that can be shortened to *Dick?*" or "What was going through my head when I decided to specialize in impotence?"

a clever name like Rustit (RUtting STallion spIT), testosterone refills are making their way into the mainstream.

"Bottoms up!" Dr. Malcolm ("I'm British and Don't Need a Silly Nickname"?) Carruthers all but says to middle-aged males at his Hormonal Healthcare Centre in London. Into these men's willing buttocks Dr. Carruthers injects pellets that slowly send testosterone throughout their system over six months' time—kind of like a hormonal layaway plan. Not only do the men feel peppier after a visit to the Centre, but they have the energy to go around changing *all* words that end in "er" to "re." The condition is irreversible.

Usually, though, testosterone is given as a straight injection every two to four weeks. And the results are just as miraculous as Premarin: Recent research has shown that such booster shots can increase sex drive, short-term memory and muscular strength in healthy older men. And that can only mean a greater supply of octogenarian bellboys who'll pinch your butt, hoist your steamer trunk over one shoulder and remember to take it to Room 206.

Testosterone tablets, held in the mouth so the hormone can be absorbed into the bloodstream, may also be prescribed but can be impractical, as the tongue may also plump up to five times its resting size. Or your man might prefer to rub on testosterone gel, available in Normal, Extra Body and Hard-to-Hold formulas. But the latest entrant into the testosterone sweepstakes is a transdermal testosterone patch. It works rather like a nicotine patch, except that, if it's doing its job, you'll both want a cigarette afterward. Unfortunately, the patch must be worn on the scrotum, and when it needs to be removed and replaced, you may find your man's screaming more unbearable than his andropausal symptoms.

So, hormone replacement is not for everyone. In fact, as Dr. Dick Spark implied at the beginning of this chapter, your man may be a little put off by the side effect: prostate cancer. Also, testosterone treatment may cause his testes to stop producing their own hormone and shrink to the size of Raisinettes, which may throw off his balance.

You can help your man find more natural ways to restore his testosterone and cope with other andropausal problems before they really get on your nerves. The following strategies can be performed almost safely.

TO MAKE HIM FEEL . . . MORE VIRILE

• *Let him win at tennis.* A study at the University of Nebraska showed that testosterone levels in varsity tennis players suddenly increased right after they were victorious in a match. Their levels dropped, however, after the varsity *football* players taunted them for wearing those sissy white outfits.

• *But first, bet him $100.* Another study found that testosterone rose in competitive tennis players who won a $100 prize. The conclusion was that those who boost their status through their own efforts, on the court or elsewhere, also elevate their hormone levels, which leads them to propose to Brooke Shields.

• *Put him through medical school again.* Dr. Alan ("The Laser"?) Mazur, a Syracuse University sociologist, noted that men's testosterone levels jumped in the hours after they were awarded their M.D. degrees. Conversely, the hormone plummeted in the only guy who received a Ph.D. in library science.

• *Don't let him join the ROTC.* Testosterone levels take a nosedive during the first weeks of officer-training school.

• *Encourage him to test-drive a tiny car with a big price tag.* He doesn't have to buy it, but gee, what's stopping him? Let the kids work their way through college like he did.

• *Buy him only expensive, imported cigars.* The cheap drugstore cigars often contain saltpeter—a preservative and libido inhibitor rumored to have been mixed into the food on military bases and in prisons to prevent "fraternizing."

• *Plan a romantic week for just the two of you at Club Med.* Don't forget to pack your *sexiest* flannel nightgown. (Just be sure to inquire about any senior-citizen discounts.)

•*Paste a picture of Mel Gibson at eye-level on every mirror in the house.* That may not fool him, but it should certainly cheer *you* up.

•*Snuggle up to him in the morning and murmur, "You were incredible last night."* Of course, what was incredible was how a human being could snore that loudly without rupturing his septum. He'll think you're talking about his sexual prowess. He will strut proudly all day, though he won't admit he can't remember doing anything.

•*Run a warm, scented bath.* Then get into it with a cup of ginseng tea and hand *him* a bottle of tequila.

. . . LESS BALD

•*Encourage him to lose weight.* As his head slims down, the remaining hair will become more compact, giving the illusion of thickness.

•*Encourage him to exercise.* It could increase the blood circulation to his scalp and slow hair loss. Working out won't bring his hair back, but you can point out you'd rather make love to a balding stud muffin (say, Sean Connery) than to a fully maned pork butt (say, Norm from *Cheers*).[68]

•*Pick him up Rogaine by the case at Price Club.* Then eliminate a few steps by pouring it directly down the bathtub drain.

•*Pretend he is Aladdin.* I heard of a fellow who wears a turban to bed because he thinks it keeps his hair from falling out during the night. (He should try wearing it during the day, so no one could tell even if it didn't.) After wrapping up his head, rub his magic lamp and make a wish that his hair comes back.

•*Shave his chest.* Another fellow swears this diverts his body's hair-making energies to other areas, and I never argue with a man who can braid his knuckles.

---

[68]And I mean that, if you're reading this, Sean.

•*Give his head a hot wax, buffing vigorously.* Supposedly heat and friction make hair grow faster and thicker. Just be sure to do it in the shade and when rain isn't expected for a few days.

•*Tell him about a study that showed college students viewed hairless men as mature and powerful.* In other words, *leaders.* Think of Winston Churchill, Moishe Dyan, Mr. Clean. They probably had their pick of coeds.

•*Remind him that balding does not occur in castrated men.* He can take this as a reassurance of his manliness or as a threat from you, if he doesn't stop whining about his hair loss. Either way, you've made your point.

. . . LESS OLD

•*Give him an at-home face-lift.* While he is sleeping, stretch his skin back from his face and secure it behind his ears with duct tape.

•*Buy him wraparound bifocals.*

•*Buy him a motorcycle, with airbags.* Be sure the kickstand is well lubricated or he'll slip a disk before he's mounted it.

•*Take two pairs of men's briefs,* one in size 32, the other in his real size—let's say, 42. Remove size labels from both; discard size 42 label. Sew size 32 label into size 42 briefs and leave in his underwear drawer. Gift wrap the size 32 briefs and tell him it's a chamois for his Corvette.

•*Invite his former high school buddies over.* Be sure to leave them plenty of refreshments, like Cajun pork rinds, 5-alarm chili and a sausage-and-peppers pizza. They'll begin the evening reminiscing about their old sports triumphs and sexual conquests, but by the end they'll be competing for the Tagamet.

•*Pick up Pat Boone's new CD,* No More Mr. Nice Guy. Dressed only in a black leather vest and studded choker, his gray chest hairs exposed, Pat treats us to his renditions of some heavy-metal classics. Nothing your man does in midlife could be as excruciatingly embarrassing as Boone's Muzak-like rendition of "Smoke on the Water."

• *Sign him up for cryogenics.* In fact, have him freeze-dried *now*, until a cure for andropause is found. In the meantime, you can live out the rest of your life in peace.

When all else fails, try this home remedy:

> **1.** Heat your oven to 350°F. Lightly grease an 8-inch-square baking pan. In a medium-sized bowl, combine 1 cup unsifted all-purpose flour, $1/2$ cup granulated sugar, 3 tablespoons unsweetened cocoa powder, 2 teaspoons baking powder and $1/2$ teaspoon salt. Stir in $1/2$ cup milk, 2 tablespoons vegetable oil and 1 teaspoon vanilla extract until smooth. Fold in $1/2$ cup chocolate chips or chopped nuts. Spread batter in the greased pan.
>
> **2.** In a small bowl, combine $1/2$ cup firmly packed dark-brown sugar and 3 tablespoons cocoa powder; sprinkle over batter. Then pour $1^1/4$ cups hot, not boiling, water over batter.
>
> **3.** Bake 45 minutes or until top is crusty and bottom is thickened. Eat warm.

This brownie pudding contains medicinal properties that will have you feeling better after just a few spoonfuls. Share some with your man, if you must.

8

Caveat Bimbo:
Women Who Love Men
Who Leave Them for Younger Women
Who Make These Men
Look Like Idiots

The heart wants what the heart wants.
—Woody Allen, in a 1992 *Newsweek* interview

*Take an anatomy lesson, you putz! The heart is
a lot higher up!*
—what Mia Farrow should have written in her
1997 autobiography, *What Falls Away*

*Y*our biggest fear right now may be that your andropausal man, mourning his lost youth and vitality, will be tempted by a younger woman into a relationship that may make him feel really, really, really good for a while but will eventually cost him his house, his children and/or his televangelism empire. Bear in mind that he is feeling very vulnerable right now, and any pressure from you might be just the excuse he needs. But you can try to steer him away from any awkward entanglements—and you may even be able to do it without the use of firearms!

If he comes home praising his new 26-year-old research assistant, for instance, you can ask him questions to remind him of their age difference, subtly.[69] And that's not so easy these days. With the resurgence of polyester bellbottoms and the emergence of *Nick at Nite*, the fashions and TV shows of the '60s and '70s have become cultural reference points for two generations, 30 years apart. Jim Morrison's Paris grave is visited by kids whose parents hadn't even met before he died.

In truth, the nostalgia hawked to baby boomers but embraced by the young adults of today seems so out of context that any day now someone from Generation X will produce a snack food called Ho Chi Minh Trail Mix. So you may have to dig a little deeper to prove to your man that he has nothing in common with anyone born after 1960:

1. Can she spell Jimi Hendrix?
2. Does she know who the Ben & Jerry's ice-cream flavor Cherry Garcia was named after?
3. Were the Watergate hearings aired during her afternoon nap?
4. Does she think *Naked Lunch* means a Caesar salad without the dressing, or that *The Making of the President* is Gennifer Flowers' autobiography?
5. Can she name a Mouseketeer *other than* Annette?
6. Does she wear tie-dyed T-shirts that she made herself in the basement with a box of Rit and a handful of rubber bands, or did she charge them at The Gap?
7. If he told her that his number came up when he was 18, does she think he still has some of the lottery money left?
8. When he told her he went to Canada to avoid the draft, did she reply, "Why didn't you just close the window"?
9. Does she think the civil rights movement won her the right to say, "Have a nice day"?
10. Does she remember when the McDonald's arches read "Over 1 Million Sold"?
11. Does she know all the words to "Louie, Louie"?
12. Does *she* know where he left his car keys?

---

[69]More subtle than, say, "Do the math—when she's *your* age, *you'll* be . . . what? Incontinent?"

BONUS MULTIPLE-CHOICE QUESTIONS

13. The fathers of Julian Lennon, Dweezil Zappa and
Jakob Dylan are:
  a. John, Paul, George and Ringo
  b. Peter, Paul and Mary
  c. John, Frank and Bob

14. *Hullabaloo, Shindig* and *Hootenanny* are:
  a. new stores at the mall
  b. Saturday morning cartoon characters
  c. the grandparents of MTV

15. Every spring:
  a. the swallows return to Capistrano
  b. a young man's fancy lightly turns to thoughts of love
  c. the California Parole Board turns down Charles
  Manson

SCORING KEY

The only acceptable answer for all, of course, is "Man, who
remembers? I was wasted from 1965 to 1973."

If you are alert, you can pick up other signals that your
man may be considering an affair. You don't even have to be
that alert—for some reason, he is so sure he will not be
caught that he will leave clues even a one-legged blood-
hound with blocked sinuses and glaucoma could track
down. In the "novel"/cookbook *Heartburn,* the betrayed
wife (played by actress Meryl Streep in the movie and by
author Nora Ephron in real life) confirms her husband's
affair by checking the telephone bills he's left in his desk
drawer. Then she makes a pie. Another real-life betrayed
wife noticed a phone-order charge for one of those cutely
named stuffed animals, like Amelia Bearheart. *She* made a
scene.[70] That's the subtle difference between real real-life
and fictional real-life.

SIGNS THAT HE MAY BE INTERESTED
IN A YOUNGER WOMAN

- Bathes more regularly.
- Bathes.
- Changes his cologne.
- Wears cologne.
- When asked to take out the garbage, he answers, "As *if!*"
- Doesn't miss an episode of *Melrose Place* or *Party of Five*.
- Buys more hairstyling products than your teenage daughter.
- Starts a diet or exercise program without any obvious motivation, such as a triple bypass.
- Trades in his Bermuda shorts with black socks and sandals for spandex biking shorts with black socks and sandals.
- Spends more time in Internet chat rooms than in your rec room.
- Receives mail from "Disease-Free Singles, Personals Box 395."
- Comes home with a tattoo that reads "Brittany," which is not your name or your teenage daughter's.
- In his sleep, mutters, "Tiffany," which is not your name or your teenage daughter's.
- During sex, yells out, "Courtney," which is not your name and had better not be your teenage daughter's.
- Leaves nude Polaroids of your adopted daughter on the mantelpiece for you to find.
- Calls to tell you he has to "work late," even though he's been unemployed for the last 6 months.
- Calls to tell you he has to go on an overnight "business trip," even though he is a toll collector.
- Files for divorce.

---

[70]Knowing *she* had never received such a gift, she called the company and the sympathic sales rep gave her the name and address of the other woman, whom she confronted. Too bad she didn't call 1-800-POISONTHESLUT instead, then she might have had a teddy named after her, perhaps "Lucrezia Beargia."

In preserving the sanctity of your marriage, never has your work been harder nor the stakes higher. Besides the usual parade of gold diggers, airheads and jailbait, a new breed of bimbo has emerged over the last few decades: the Beautiful Intelligent Media-savvy Business-minded Opportunist—or *B.I.M.B.O.*

In the good old days, a woman caught fooling around with a married man would have had the decency to take her own life, or at least the first bus out of town. In these more scandal-tolerant times, homewreckers are often rewarded with a lucrative jeans-modeling contract, the starring role in a Broadway show, a pictorial in *Playboy,* the bulk of his baby-care-products fortune or control of his share of the Beatles' royalties. *Your* only recourse may be to sell your story to the *National Enquirer,* write a tell-all book, start your own magazine, testify before the grand jury or appear on *60 Minutes.* He'll just look like an idiot as the media speculates over whether he's impotent, senile, guilty of the statutory-rape charges or facing Chapter 11. So don't worry. Everybody makes out.

Still, you may have grown fond of your husband over the years and want to hold on to him a little longer, in the hope that he—or his portfolio of treasury bonds—matures. Of course, if he's just celebrated his 10th anniversary or third child with his new wife, it's time you contested your prenuptial agreement and moved on.

But this *could* be a passing phase. Often he just wants to forget his past and give himself a fresh start. Since *he* hasn't really changed, though, his lover will eventually pass him right back to you. Modern young women are not as tolerant as our generation. Former comedian David Steinberg, separated from his wife of 22 years, recently admitted to Tom Snyder on *The Late Late Show,* "Women these days are different from when I was dating in my 30s. They want orgasms."

While you may feel you can't compete with someone who still dabs Clearasil on every night, you do have time, experience, the kids and community-property law on your side. Also, remember that a younger woman is usually attracted to an older man because she assumes he has more money, power and stability than a man her own age. When she finds out none of that is true, she dumps him. An older man is attracted to a younger woman because he assumes she is not *you.* You can change that assumption by becoming *her.* So swallow your pride and, with no apologies to Ellen Fein and Sherrie Schneider, authors of *The Rules: Time-Tested Secrets to Capturing the Heart of Mr. Right,* follow these 10 simple strategies:

THE FOOLS:
UNTESTED SECRETS FOR RECAPTURING THE HEART OF
MR. GOOD-ENOUGH

RULE #1 *Be a "Creature Unlike Any Mother."*

After your years of marriage and raising children, your man has begun viewing you as a maternal figure. He's had it with you nagging him to remember his appointments, his car inspections or his blood-pressure medication. So stop taking responsibility for him! When he fails to show up at his IRS audit, is ticketed for driving an expired vehicle or has a massive stroke, he'll thank you for it. And whatever you do, don't clip coupons.

RULE #2 *Stare at Him, and Talk Too Much, But Only About Him.*

One thing a middle-aged man finds so alluring about a young woman is how wonderful she thinks he is. So look up to him, even if that means you have to stand in a hole. When you're in public, gaze at him adoringly and when he asks you what you're looking at, blush and say, "Oh, nothing." Never point out that he has a sample of every item on the salad bar stuck between his teeth. Tell him endlessly that he's strong and masculine and smart and taller than he actually is. Never contradict him, even in situations that might result in decapitation—though it may be okay to give your opinion in the form of a question, so he thinks it's his idea, such as, "Do you think that underpass is a little low for this monster truck?" Laugh at all his jokes, even if they're old enough to have appeared as glyphs in Tutankhamen's tomb or been around the block enough times to have earned frequent-flier miles to Rangoon.

RULE #3 *Meet Him Halfway—and Make Him Pay For It.*

If he's looking for a more youthful and attractive partner, give him one. Have your face peeled, your boobs siliconed, your tummy tucked, your teeth bonded and your thighs vacuumed out. Dip into his retirement fund to foot the bill. Answer all his questions with "Like, totally!" Cancel *Mirabella;* subscribe to *Seventeen.* Give up your demanding catering business—though the second income pays the mortgage on your beach house—so that he will not feel threatened by your success and your time away from him. Instead, become a minor avant-garde artist, a minor actress, a minor model or just a minor who sponges off him because looking for a real job would mess up her manicure.

RULE #4 *See Him More than Once or Twice a Month.*

Your separate interests and hectic lives may have caused the two of you to drift apart. So plan more time together. Drop in at his office unexpectedly, such as just as the door closes behind him and his secretary. Surprise him by showing up in the plane seat next to him on his St. Croix junket, saying, "Wasn't it sweet of Lolita to give me her ticket? By the way, her doctor says she won't be able to do any typing for at least 6 weeks."

RULE #5 *Don't Call Him . . . to Account.*

An andropausal man often feels his wife knows too much about him—he feels he will always be judged by his past mistakes. So clean the slate. Forget about the time he was so caught up carousing with his buddies that he missed your honeymoon cruise. Forget about the time he borrowed your inheritance to back a 50-to-1 shot at Hialeah. Forget about the time he went golfing while you had brain surgery. If you can't forget, you might want to have someone hit you repeatedly on the back of the head until amnesia sets in.

RULE #6 *Don't Open Up Too Fast. His Beer, That Is.*

Lift the pop-top real slow, until you have him begging for it.

RULE #7 *Be Dishonest.*

The last thing he wants from you right now is the truth. Why would he want to hear that he's a balding, out-of-shape, prematurely ejaculating failure? Save that for his eulogy. For now, squeeze his imaginary muscles. Run your fingers through his imaginary hair. Tell him he hasn't lost it, even if you can't remember what "it" used to look like.

RULE # 8 *Stop Hating Him If He Doesn't Buy You a Romantic Gift for Your Birthday or Valentine's Day.*

Don't show so much interest in material things—after all, his young love would be thrilled with merely a single rose or a pack of gum. (Or so she says, as she squeals with delight over the diamond tennis bracelet he's brought her.) If he gives you an air freshener from the car wash for your 25th anniversary, consider it as precious as "White Diamonds." Squeal with delight. If he gets you the same thing next year, have them made into earrings. Wear them proudly. Later, you can cash in his CDs and buy yourself something you really want.

RULE #9 *Don't Involve Him in Your Family—or His.*

As he faces his own mortality, your man finds he can't cope with his growing children or his aging parents. Not that he ever kept in touch with them himself—if only *you* didn't insist he show up at holidays. His young divorcée would never bother him with her day-care problems and *can't* bring him home to meet her folks. So do what you can to unknot your family ties. When he does ask about the kids, say, "Kids? What kids? Oh, those. They're not ours. I'm just baby-sitting." For the first time since you've been married, forget to send a birthday card to his mother—he'll be grateful when she stops speaking to him. When he's called away from work to post bail for his father, who's been arrested for indecent exposure, say, "Oh, yes. The nursing home phoned last week to say he escaped. I didn't want to worry you."

RULE #10 *If You Read[71] a Book About Male Menopause, Reassure Him That None of It Applies to Him.*

---

[71]**Or Write.**

Backword

*T*o mark your rite of passage through your husband's andropause, you arrange to go off with your man alone for a few days in the mountains. You want to honor your renewed commitment to your marriage, chart the path that will guide you toward growing old together gracefully and reflect on how you've learned to accept each other's weaknesses during this trying time. Now that the incident with that waitress at the pancake house is behind him, you can both be thankful that she didn't press charges.

You arrive at the rustic cabin just as the inflamed tip of the sun plunges between the provocatively undulating hills while the moon tentatively wraps her pearlized fingers around the pinnacle behind you. In the scattering light, you shudder delicately, then turn and trip over the luggage he left on the porch when he went inside to start a woodfire. As the room fills with smoke and robust swearing, you teasingly suggest that he has built a blaze hot enough for a crematorium. In the ancient Hindu custom of suttee, he reminds you with a chuckle, a grief-stricken widow was burned alive and often involuntarily. You banter good-naturedly this way for a while until one of you stomps off to bed.

The next morning you awake after a rejuvenating sleep and draw apart the tatty curtains to behold a dazzling sight: the rugged landscape has been blanketed by a dusting of snow, about two feet, completely filling the open "clamshell" still strapped to the roof of your Volvo. Soon you also discover the thick rime of frost in the toilet—unusual for a Fourth of July weekend, you muse before diving back into bed and pushing him out to rebuild the fire.

Cooking on the hearth, you feel an overwhelming kinship to the pioneer women who had traveled this route before you. They too had drawn strength from the untamed mountains after leaving behind their predictable lives. They chose to start anew in an unknown territory and set out with great faith in the future, only to find that they were members of the Donner party.

Rousing yourself from your reverie, you serve your husband as he lights his third cigarette of the morning in defiance of his promise to cut down. The hearty breakfast fuels your bodies, your souls and a lively debate over who forgot to tell whom to buy propane for the cookstove. After a while, you settle into a companionable silence. Then he picks a glowing ember from his plate and observes wryly that this will be the first time he's ever gotten a splinter from eating pancakes. The spirited discussion resumes.

Later, when the pipes have unfrozen, you tempt him into the shower with an invitation to wash the soot off his scalp. After languidly lathering each other in the bracing spray, you pull him close and let out a moan from deep within you as the hot water runs out and an icy freshet cascades down your spine.

Then clad in matching Stewart-plaid flannel shirts and Thinsulate anoraks from last winter's L.L. Bean closeout, you are drawn outdoors by the heady scent of pine. You hold hands as the crisp air slaps your face, concusses your lungs and petrifies your nosehairs. How good it feels to be alive!

Once the Motor Club has jump-started the Volvo, you head into town for a cozy lunch at a streamside cafe. You note an elderly couple at the next table, snowy hair framing their radiant faces, his gnarled finger lightly caressing her wrinkled pink cheek. After all these years, they're still so much in love, you think, until the woman's husband comes back from the men's room and grabs his old fishing buddy by the throat and yells at him to stop manhandling his wife.

As they settle their dispute, you and your husband sidle past the sheriff's cruiser to your car, ready for another life-affirming adventure. On the way back to the cabin, your man pulls over—he shouldn't have had four cups of coffee with lunch!—and does his business as you admire the breathtaking panorama. If only every day could be like this.

Having accidentally backed the car into a snowbank, he suggests a refreshing hike, as the steadily growing breeze sends his baseball cap spinning down the mountainside. A misstep off the trail leads you serendipitously into a tree-canopied glade. Here, the ground is still verdant with wild herbs and your senses pick up the pungency of sage, the piquancy of mustard, the perspicuity of turmeric, and what is that? Peppermint? he guesses, twirling the leaves between his fingers. Poison ivy, you realize.

Walking and scratching together up the spiraling path of the mountain, you think how far you've both come. As if he were reading your mind, he suddenly turns to you, takes you in his arms and thanks you for sticking with him through the lean years, the colicky years, the Reagan years. His gratitude for your role as his life partner knows no bounds. He wants you to know that you have always been the perfect wife, mother and friend. Any problems in your marriage were his fault. Knowing this, he says, he won't contest anything you ask for in the divorce settlement.

Standing on the narrow precipice, the snow swirling about your ankles, all at once you feel an overwhelming surge of energy. Hot, vibrating, explosive, it shoots upward, sending these words buzzing through your head: If I do it now, the forest rangers won't find his body until spring. By then, I'll have cleaned out the joint account and been long gone to Antigua.

You step back and smile. As you rush forward with your hands thrust before you, your heart fills with a profound peace.